Judy Cornwell was born in London and brought up in Australia and Sussex. She is one of Britain's leading actresses, whose stage career spans the Joan Littlewood Theatre Workshop, the RSC, the West End and the acclaimed 1993 national tour of *The Cemetary Club*. Her most recent international film was *Santa Claus - The Movie*. Her countless TV performances include the phenomenally successful BBC comedy series, *Keeping Up Appearances*. *Cow and Cow Parsley* is her first novel, first published in 1985, and her subsequent novels are *Fishcakes at the Ritz* and *The Seventh Sunrise*.

Judy Cornwell is married to the broadcaster and journalist, John Parry. They have one son, Edward, and live in Brighton.

COW AND COW PARSLEY

JUDY CORNWELL

POCKET
BOOKS

LONDON · SYDNEY · NEW YORK · TOKYO · SINGAPORE · TORONTO

First published in Great Britain by Seagull Books, 1985
First published in Pocket Books, 1995
An imprint of Simon & Schuster Ltd
A Paramount Communications Company

Simon & Schuster Ltd
West Garden Place
Kendal Street
London W2 2AQ

Simon & Schuster of Australia Pty Ltd
Sydney

A CIP catalogue record for this book is available
from the British Library.

ISBN 0-671-85386-4

Printed and bound in Great Britain by
HarperCollins, Manufacturing.

CONTENTS

PROLOGUE

In the universe, Dagda, the Lord af all knowledge and King of the Tuatha de Danaan, rested after another skirmish with the powers of darkness.

His wise old head listened as the faint cries of his daughters, "the Brigit", echoed through time.

He stirred as the three sisters' sound summoned him to earth.

They stood on the hill top, calling Him.

Brigantia's body was old, it was time for it to die and her spirit to find a new one.

Belisima's body was middle-aged, she still had time to instruct the younger Bridget in the crafts before she, too, passed away from her shell to be reborn again.

Young Bridget was only twenty-two. Her sparkling eyes radiated energy, and her mane of red hair streamed in the wind as she gave all her youthful strength in supporting the older women against the stormy elements.

In this body, it was to be her first experience of union with Dagda. Her searching soul had found her two sisters waiting for her and after time for preparation and instruction, the sound of the "Brigit" was now possible.

His presence filtered through the etheric membrane around the earth and bore down towards the "Brigit".

His love swirled round them in a protective mist, moving the direction of the forceful wind. He breathed warmth into their chilled bones and kissed their minds with poetry and music.

He took away all fear and shared with them a glimpse of divine truth.

As he drew away from the earth, he felt the warm smile of his brother Lugh, defender of the Tuatha, and heard the curiosity of his son MacOc, protector in darkness.

He sent his sound through eternity to his mother, Danaan, asking her to spare the world.

He was told, gently, not to question the Divine order.

CHAPTER ONE

The ginger tom licked its lips, smoothed its whiskers, and languidly surveyed its morning's work. The bone, lying amongst the tattered strips of the grey plastic refuse bag, was licked clean.

A south-westerly wind sneaked up behind him and maliciously combed his fur backwards with its icy January fingers. Shuddering with discomfort, yet attempting to retain his dignity, the cat moved deftly around the side of Number Eight, Clifton Villas. Sheltered from the wind, he moved more slowly, rubbing his back along the thick Victorian walls, then, after padding over the frozen moss and lichen he crouched, assessing the distance between the ivy-covered fence and the ground.

A lonely piece of forgotten Christmas tinsel twisted and glittered as the wind changed its direction and pursued the cat. It howled savagely through the knots of ivy as the cat leapt on to the wooden fence. Nimbly, he scampered along to the adjoining high wall that enclosed the adjacent gardens. Another leap and he was sheltered by the elegant bulk of Numbers Seven and Eight.

From his lofty position the cat gazed down the row of small stuccoed houses that sloped gently towards the beach. Through the gentle early morning noises came the distant sound of the sea being pulled through the shingle, as the wind heaved the waves on to the Brighton sea shore and the ocean reclaimed them.

The sparrows, huddling around the pyrex dish of water and scattered Mother's Pride crumbs put out for them by the ever-caring Mrs. Robinson of Number Six, watched anxiously as the ginger tom scrabbled along the wall, trying to regain his balance against the gusts of wind blowing between the semi-detached houses.

Inside Number Five Mrs. Kingman's Sealyham, peering through the kitchen window, barked with rage when he saw his old enemy walking regally past his territory.

Echoing howls and yapping came from the spaniel at Number Four and the Cairn at Number Three.

Again the cat reeled from the blast of salt air that howled through the gap between Five and Four but, like an experienced trapeze artist, he recovered his poise and continued on his route.

As he approached Number Three he stiffened. A middle-aged woman in a blue fluffy dressing gown was standing, quite still, in front of her closed back door.

Behind her, from inside the house, came muffled screams of anger from the Cairn.

The tom's fur, already blown backwards by the wind, rose higher as he sensed danger. The woman turned and looked casually towards the stark cherry tree. The cat's tension eased and he started again along the wall.

Suddenly, the woman moved quickly. In her hand she held a silver object. The cat crouched defensively in the centre of the wall. A wave of water knocked him off his perch into the back yard of a poky boarding house in the next street.

Isabelle stood triumphant in the middle of the lawn and raised her saucepan in a warrior-like salute to the neighbouring audience, hidden by net curtains.

"One down, five hundred to go!" she bawled, then, stepping carefully round the Cairn turds, she ran for central-heated protection.

As she opened the back door, Mac, the Cairn, pushed past her and ran frantically into the garden to look for the ginger enemy.

Alternatively peeing and yapping he vented his fury at the south-west wind that teased him by mewling through the forsythia bush. Isabelle chuckled as she watched Mac's antics in the garden. Professor McAnally and his wife Audrey, from Number Two, had both missed the cat yesterday. They had tried with the weedkiller spray and a pudding basin. She hoped they had observed her successful bullseye.

The eight o'clock news reader on Radio Four was a woman with a sibilant 's'. She was having great difficulties with "South Africa's racialist policies". Isabelle listened to her lisping and slobbering as she made some coffee and warmed herself over the

Aga, then realising that she hadn't followed any of the news items switched the offending voice off and took her coffee through to the lounge and sat on her favourite green leather chesterfield by the bow windows.

The room overlooked a small front rose garden. Iron work railings around the small balcony, overhung by a deep canopy, made it easy for Isabelle to sit, discreetly hidden from view, while she watched the "morning people" walk down Clifton Villas. A punk disciple, a tenant living in Number Five's basement, tottered down the street in obviously uncomfortable shoes, her pink and green striped hair spikily waving in the wind like jagged grass.

Some children who attended the local Roman Catholic primary school leant their small frames against the wind and laughed defiantly at the cold weather. They were sturdy, well-fed and warmly dressed with faces pink from the icy wind. Behind them struggled a shabbier child, clutching an inadequate trendy jerkin round him. He was eating a chocolate bar and wore the worried expression of an enforced loner.

Isabelle felt a surge of pity for the small tired face resting on such a tiny body and she shivered in sympathy.

An old railway porter from Brighton station started to walk slowly down the hill. Behind him, by one of the elms that lined the Villas, his old mongrel with a drooping belly tried valiantly to mark his territory. It would take him fifteen minutes to get to the end of the street, she thought, watching the sandy-haired old dog fighting the wind and his arthritis.

Isabelle opened her letters. The first was an invitation from the Sussex Galleries to Mr. and Mrs. C. Carrington. There was going to be a showing of new local artists on the twenty-third of January, between six and seven thirty, wine and cheese.

Isabelle sipped her coffee and pulled her cigarettes and lighter from her dressing gown pocket.

She'd bought "Cow and Cow Parsley" from the Sussex Galleries for Chris for his birthday.

She had loved the gallery. It was such an unpretentious place. The people neither tried to sell her anything nor praise her obviously amateur appreciation. They had just let her browse happily among the familiar Sussex landscapes, abstract thoughts, and nudes reclining on wooden chairs in modest flatlets.

She had been wondering about the nudes, which Brighton girls had been the models, possibly daughters of her friends, and whether they had been having affairs with the artists. When she had first seen "Cow and Cow Parsley", it was the colours that attracted her. Soft splashes of sage green and cream with brown patches and speckles. It was only when she drew closer to the painting that she realised that she was seeing a large contented cow through a haze of cow parsley. Childhood memories flooded her emotions. Memories, of lying in a daisy-covered field and trying to see the world from a bee's point of view, re-awakened feelings that she had long ceased experiencing, a sense of anticipation, and a feeling of being at one with the earth.

She had bought the painting, hoping that she could share it all with Chris. As he had unwrapped it he had complimented her on her taste and then said, "We should buy more of this young artist's work, it will probably be worth something in twenty years time."

As Isabelle felt the familiar loneliness and emptiness return she told herself that it was just the way his lawyer's mind worked. He couldn't help it, but for her own survival she pushed the feelings that had so thrilled her back into the recesses of her mind, into her emotional file for sensitivities to be protected and not shared.

Mac's whines and scratches at the back door pulled Isabelle out of her reverie in time to see the railway porter's dog cock his leg against the last elm in the street.

"Coming, Mac dog, coming."

As Isabelle shuffled along the hall to the back door she could hear the dog grumbling at having been forgotten. He walked inside stiffly, like a clockwork toy, glared at her with disgust and made for his biscuit bowl.

"I'm sorry," she crooned, attempting to win back his favour. A muffled growl came from the bowl.

The second letter was a dentist's bill. Harley Street really was becoming expensive these days, she thought, looking at the elaborate scripting on the thick creamy paper.

A letter from Marcus told her how he thought rugger was

barbaric, and cross-country runs in this weather was unnecessary cruelty to children. He enclosed two tickets for HMS Pinafore, his school play.

"Why can't I go to a comprehesive, where the teachers go on strike?" he had written. "These Hurstwood College chaps see that you're active all the time."

"Character building," Chris would say. "Haven't you noticed in the city the chaps never need overcoats. Good, tough schooling. It's the others who need the raincoats and scarves."

"Balls," Isabelle said out loud. Although she would never say it to Chris.

How she missed Marcus and yearned for the exeats and long holidays when they would be together to chat, plot and share secrets. Drying his hair in front of the log fire she would watch the damp auburn slowly turn to red-gold threads. Even though he was now fifteen, when sitting in his pyjamas he still had that childish innocence that he used to have when she rocked him to sleep in her arms.

Sometimes, she wished that she'd been stronger and stopped Chris from sending him to boarding school, but seeing the argument from Chris' point of view, yes, she probably would have mollycoddled Marcus and hindered him with her possessiveness.

She also saw the benefits of public school education at the end of the holidays when she was worn out after her effort to be the perfect mother. At forty-eight it was pleasant to occasionally nap in the afternoons instead of rushing about at four o'clock as she had done during prep school days.

A pleasant stirring in the bowels, the result of a bowl of muesli, two cups of coffee and two cigarettes, reminded Isabelle, as she rushed upstairs to the bathroom, to bless the benefits of nicotine.

Surely the scales were wrong.

Bathed, dried and rubbed in vitamin E oil, Isabelle tried to stop wobbling as she squinted at the faded pound mark. It could't be. Unable to believe the result from her view, five feet, five inches above the machine, she attempted a crouching position. Her stomach got in the way of her knees, forcing her into a frog-like squat.

Eleven and a half stone.

5

She stood up, knees clicking and spine cracking and glared at the middle-aged shell reflected in the mirror. How had this squishy blubber dared to spring up so suddenly to encase her youth like this? Even her bottom had drooped since Christmas and her thighs looked like the seaweed that she liked to squash on Brighton beach. What was the new word for it? Cellulite, that was it.

Covering the offending body with her fluffy dressing gown, she lit a cigarette and stared at the reflected image in the mirror. It had happened so quickly. All the grey hairs, and dear God, was it? No, surely it was a trick of the light.

She fled to the magnified shaving mirror in the bathroom. It was sticking out like a cat's whisker from her chin.

Isabelle blushed with shame. How long had it been there for all the world to see?

"God's vengence for being cruel to stray cats," she babbled to herself, squinting as she tried to manipulate the tweezers around the offending grey hair.

Mac, thinking that Isabelle had called him, padded into the bathroom. Seeing her preoccupied he masturbated with the bath mat.

"Got it!" Isabelle shouted triumphantly.

The dog froze, halfway to canine heaven.

"Oh, for God's sake Mac." Isabelle looked at the guiltily crouching Cairn.

An answering growl reminded her that nature rules O.K.

"Bloody wanker," she said crossly, returning to the bedroom.

The dog bit his towelling mate and continued happily.

The jacket potatoes were nearly cooked, the salad was tossed and the Wiener schnitzel slowly turned a golden brown. Isabelle cut the soda bread and arranged it in the straw basket.

"The marvellous thing about the end of a love affair is one's phone bills go down." Daphne nursed her gin and tonic. Isabelle was deep in thought about Daphne's affair.

She had first met Daphne when they had both been eight and a half months pregnant. Isabelle had been a five foot five, thirteen stone and Daphne had been an elegant five foot eight, ten and half stone with a gentle curve. Isabelle had waddled up to Daphne, her bellybutton leading by a good ten inches and they'd both dissolved into helpless giggles.

Two weeks later, Daphne had produced Emma and three days later, Marcus arrived.

Daphne was a beautiful Welsh redhead. The occasional grey hair that dared to appear was quickly yanked out or was red like the others by the following day.

Orphaned at ten, brought up in a good Welsh boarding school with money in trust, she was a natural leader of women. Isabelle would glow from her reflected vivacity.

Chris always knew when she'd spent a day with her "noisy friend" because she'd become a bit "uppity" as he called it.

After a gentle year at Cambridge Daphne had played at the modelling scene and then married an American film producer who admired the "quaint architecture" in Britain. They were known as great party givers and because of Isabelle and Daphne's nursery and playgroup friendship, she and Chris had been introduced into their social circle.

Daphne had been most impressed by Chris and Isabelle often suspected that she wondered how she had landed him. Although she had never implied as much, she was too loyal a friend for that sort of behaviour.

Chris had dismissed Daphne's husband as "obviously second generation mafia" and the people at the parties as "phoney, nouveau-riche shirtmakers".

Isabelle noticed he still appreciated the very low cut evening gowns worn by the shirtmaker's wives.

After the first party she had gone out and bought a similar dress. A black, backless, plunging piece of crepe and she had worn it on the next invitation. She'd stood most of the evening feeling very uncomfortable, despite the Playtex. Apart from a few black looks Chris had ignored her at the party but afterwards, at home, over cocoa, he'd said, "Don't buy anything as silly as that again. You're just not the type. Yours arms are too long for a start."

Isabelle had sadly put the dress away, feeling like an

orangutang.

Daphne preened at her reflection in the glass kitchen cabinet. "Mind you, I've lost weight. Love affairs make you lose weight, that's one good thing."

Isabelle tried to pull in her stomach in sympathy with Daphne's philosophy but developed wind so she concentrated on the Wiener schnitzel. "God, that looks good." Daphne peered over Isabelle's shoulder, filling the surrounding space with the scent of Chloe. "Nearly ready." Isabelle tossed the veal once more.

"But the end of an affair," Daphne prowled around the kitchen table and broke off some more soda bread, "gives enormous freedom. You know Isabelle, no more frenzy about how long it will last, it's over."

As Isabelle served up the food, she wondered whether it was bravado or fact. Whether Daphne was really happy living the liberated life of the divorcee. As Chris had cruelly pointed out, "The lover looks exactly the same as the film producer." As if in answer to her thought, Daphne chimed in, "Why do we always go for the same type of men, time after time?"

"Do you think we do?" asked Isabelle, chewing heartily.

"Every man I've ever gone for has been just like Tony," said Daphne. "This is wonderful, Isabelle, I haven't had real soda bread since I was in Dublin. When was that? Mmm, eighty-one. When Tony was making that dreadful Irish film, all birth control and poverty, you know the sort of thing. That's where he first met that little bitch. There you are you see."

"What?" Isabelle helped herself to more salad.

"She looks just like me, doesn't she, when I was younger? You see its the same for men."

"She isn't as pretty as you were." Isabelle thought of more loyal things to say as she shovelled more butter into her potato.

"And," she added triumphantly, "She won't wear as well as you have. You look better now than you did ten years ago."

Daphne, reassured, happily ate her potato.

Outside, the wind was still howling, yet inside the kitchen the sound of the coke shuffling inside the Aga, the clock ticking, Mac lapping his water and Daphne's murmured conversation, created a lovely cosy cocoon.

She loved being with Daphne; had never felt envious of her beauty and vivacity, just a great pride, that out of all the smart and witty women in Brighton Daphne had chosen her as friend and ally. Listening to her chattering happily, Isabelle remembered her sitting in the same chair, the previous year, when Tony had just left her. She had sat, her face swollen through crying, sipping her coffee. The object of gleeful gossip, bewildered, affronted and humiliated, she had gratefully accepted Isabelle's placid, non-competitive sanctuary.

Little Emma had regarded the whole drama with stoic sophistication but when the lover, a sexologist, looking just like Tony, appeared on the scene, she erupted with violent disapproval.

Isabelle hadn't liked him either.

With Daphne's eventual divorce, a whole new world had opened for Isabelle. Used to being left on her own for weeks at a time while Chris attended to his business in Bahrain or Dubai, Isabelle suddenly found herself with a friend, also on her own, with whom she could share visits to the cinema, art galleries and a few of her secrets.

The appearance on the scene of the sexologist had spoilt all that, so she, like Emma, welcomed the change in Daphne's circumstances.

"It was never the same after I told him that I didn't like it up the bum."

Daphne stretched out on the sofa, puffing a cigarette.

"Piles," replied Isabelle, putting another log on the fire. "Bad for the piles, I should think." She poured some more tea.

The noise of the paper boy crashing open the wrought iron gate forced Isabelle to her feet. Glancing out of the window she was in time to see the street lights come on, momentarily interrupting the creeping grey twilight.

From the town came the low hum of the homegoing traffic. Muffled figures, some carrying heavy shopping bags, wearily struggled up the hill, their breath forming wispy vapours as they spoke in voices pitched high with the cold.

"He said a lot of women like it." Daphne continued in her reverie.

"I don't." Isabelle squashed a memory that threatened the tranquil evening. "There's a good play on I.T.V. at eight o'clock. Do you want to stay and watch it?"

"The Arabs do it don't they, because they believe the next Messiah has to come from a man?" Daphne pursued her line of thought.

"I've never heard of that." Isabelle, satisfied with her planned evening's television, turned the pages of the *Evening Argus* in order to read the headlines.

"Perhaps he'll pop out of an oil well instead."

"Who?" Isabelle was engrossed in the story of the Brighton rapist who'd attacked three old ladies.

"The next Messiah."

A log shifted in the glowing fire, allowing a burst of flames to throw shadows across Daphne's face.

"Perhaps we all need a Messiah," Daphne murmured.

Isabelle wondered whether Mac would defend her, if during the night the Brighton rapist broke into the house. She looked at the hairy shadow stretched across the hearth and decided not. She would leave the porch light on when Daphne left in case he came ringing at the front door. Then she would have time to peek through the peephole and phone the police before he broke the door down with his axe. She shivered, alarmed at her own fantasy.

Would she have the courage to defend Daphne, she wondered, if she was attacked as she crossed the street to her parked car. She remembered when there had been a girl screaming late at night, during the summer, she had urged Chris to intervene. He had looked out of the window at the struggling couple and promptly phoned the police.

Isabelle had been horrified and told Chris that the girl could be murdered before the police arrived. "Nonsense," Chris had replied, "She's probably neurotic and having a row with her husband who's bound to be Irish and drunk. I have no intention of having my nose broken because of a couple of misfits."

10

He had been right. The police arrived, talked to the couple and they had silently gone their way, the man with his arm placed protectively around the subdued girl, shielding her from the watchful eyes of the complainants.

The shrill sound of the telephone interrupted her reverie. "Ask not for whom the bell tolls, it tolls for thee, 'cause nobody knows I'm here." Daphne laughed at her own wit as Isabelle crossed to the hall.

"I'm getting a few things from the office then I'll catch the six-forty. Will you meet me?"

Isabelle wished that he'd said, "Darling, I'm back. I've missed you. As soon as I got off the plane, I wanted to see you straight away."

"Are you there?"

"Yes, when did you get back?"

"Two fifteen. Bloody awful flight. Do you know, when we went through the sound barrier, my wine changed its taste. God knows what it must do to your blood."

"Probably changes to wine."

"What? Oh, I see, the communion in reverse. No, seriously, the wine smelt quite different. It can't be good for us to fly at that speed, can it? Have you some homemade vegetable soup? It's bloody cold."

"I'll make some. Seven-fifty, I'll pick you up."

"Right." The phone clicked.

Depression descended as she replaced the phone. Her whole planned evening's viewing and chat was ruined. The peaceful way of life was over until he returned to Dubai.

"Chris is back?" Daphne chirped.

Isabelle forced a look of wifely anticipation.

"Yes, and he wanted my homemade soup. He's fed up with sheep's eyes and fruit."

Daphne laughed. "Get back to your kitchen, Isabelle. I'm off."

"Give me a ring." Daphne, wrapped in red fox, looked very youthful. Her skin flushed with the smooth ruddiness of mid menopause. The smell of Chloe on fur lingered in the hall as Isabelle made her way to the kitchen.

As she chopped the carrots and onion she wondered whether

11

to dig out her dutch cap.

As the blender whizzed the stock and carrots into a fine country soup fit for homecoming husbands she remembered that the cap had perished four years ago and she'd thrown it out.

CHAPTER TWO

The train was late. Isabelle wondered whether to pollute the station and waste petrol by switching on the heater or try to last a little while longer in the cold car.

She reached under her sheepskin coat for her apron pocket and pulled out her cigarettes, matches and Polo mints.

Chris hated the stale smell of cigarettes so she wound down the window to let out the offensive smoke and shivered as the cold air crept inside the car.

A queue of commuters stood waiting miserably on the station forecourt for the occasional Streamline taxi. As the trains arrived the queue grew longer. Some of the people shuffled their feet to keep warm, others gazed intently towards the station entrance, willing the cabs to arrive.

Parked sideways to the curb, like cards lined up for a game of patience, were other cars containing other waiting wives of varying ages. Some sleek and affluent, their husbands the only missing accessory for their evening out. They shared their poised magnificence with the shivering outsiders by accentuating themselves by the cars' interior lights. Young wives fought tired toddlers. Jeans-clad students, with broken down bangers, restlessly paced in and out of the station, then returned to their cars and combed their hair.

A portly, middle-aged drunk, in animated conversation with himself, stood, swaying gently by the entrance of the station. Quite suddenly, the drunk took offence at his invisible companion and menaced the air with his umbrella. A sailor watched the antics with cynical amusement.

To end up mad on a railway station was one of Isabelle's many fears and it often helped to check her habit of talking to herself.

The thought of the soup, left on top of the Aga, forming a skin, forced Isabelle out of the car and into the cold draughty station where other people were milling around looking at the indicator board or the sullen ticket collectors, all hoping for some sign or news of the train arrivals and departures.

"How late will the London train be?" asked Isabelle.

The ticket collector chewed the inside of his cheek and remained silent. Isabelle would have liked to have given him a karate chop on the side of his swollen, purple neck, that is if she had known how to give a karate chop. Sensing her mounting aggression, he turned and stared defiantly at her with his sunken, watery eyes. "How would I know? Could be ten minutes, could be 'alf an 'ar."

Muttering to herself, Isabelle joined the other frustrated people, adding another audible sound to the symphony of revolution on Brighton station. A high-pitched whine created a lull in the crowd's jabbering, then an incomprehensible burble from the tannoy announced the arrival of the London train. The crowd surged forward to meet the gabbling, rushing mass disgorged from the electric train.

He was a head above other men. His eyes piercing blue against his tanned skin. Amongst the scrambling, dark clothed commuters, he looked, with his fair, greying hair, like Lawrence of Arabia on the wrong film set.

"Like a bloody cattle truck, bloody inefficient, incompetent bastards," he said, as he hugged her briefly.

His taut, athletic body made her feel like a soft blancmange.

"How are you, Bumble?" Before she could reply, he ranted on. "You'd think that the British would be used to a smattering of snow, wouldn't you? But oh, no, as soon as the temperature drops, the country comes to a bloody standstill."

"I think it's a go slow," she suggested as she helped to carry his bags to the car.

"They all smell. God, is Britain so impoverished that the people can't afford to have their clothes clean and take a bath?"

"Dry cleaning is very expensive now," she said, closing the boot of the car.

As she drove him home, snowflakes swirled and scurried in the wind. Turning into the Villas, they danced in front of her headlights, then fell gracefully to form eddies across the road, resembling the beach at low tide.

"This country is disintegrating, Isabelle," said Chris. "Every time I come home I expect to find England as it used to be but all I see is further decay."

As she turned into the driveway laughing punk rockers chased past the house, their rasping croaks assaulting the stillness of the Villas as they barged their way through the wind.

Chris stood by the gate watching them as if they were Martians. "It's like the Weimar Republic all over again," he said.

The warm air from the hall rushed to meet them. "Hello Machiavelli."

Why did he always pat Mac as if he were an Alsatian, she wondered, as she ladled the soup. It always brought squeals of protest from the little dog who would sensibly disappear under the sofa until Christopher's large frame seemed to be in a state of repose.

"Would you like to open a bottle of wine, Chris?" she asked, desperately trying to recreate the homely peacefulness, now shattered by his energetic presence.

"On Victoria Station I shared the fumes of a million multinational farts, all originating from various brews. I think it's quite put me off a bottle of wine," he replied mournfully.

The idea of Chris, standing on Victoria Station, surrounded by the smelly people, was too much for Isabelle and she started to giggle helplessly, clutching at the Aga for some support against falling onto the floor. Chris joined in and there, in the warmth of the kitchen, there was a delicious moment of comradeship against the unfriendly world.

After the duty-free cigarettes and Capricci had been brought out she apologised for the soda bread but explained that owing to the lorry drivers' strike there was a bread shortage and she'd been unable to get wholemeal. Chris said nothing but assumed an air of resignation and apart from a few questions about Marcus and household bills, ate the rest of the meal in silence.

She cleared the dining room table quietly. Chris was frowning with concentration as he folded and refolded his napkin, his face reflecting his changing thoughts. Isabelle wondered what was worrying him. It couldn't be over the soda bread she thought as she filled the coffee pot. Perhaps it was something to do with his work.

"Is anything wrong, Chris?" she asked, returning to the dining room. Abruptly, he got up from the table and went into the hall where she could hear him unlocking his briefcase.

"Bring the coffee to the lounge, Isabelle. We've got to have a serious talk."

He was usually disgruntled after a long flight. She wondered what he was going to sound off about this time. She hadn't been extravagant and the telephone bill was much lower than all her friends' accounts. The school fees had gone up again but that shouldn't worry him too much.

He was standing by the fire, staring intently into space. Sibelius' Karelia Suite was his chosen background to whatever dramatic offering he was about to produce. She poured the coffee, watching him carefully and remembering his grumbles about the Concord.

"I want to sell up and move into the country," he announced.

"Mmm," replied Isabelle, handing him his coffee. He was going through another phase of wanting to become a Moslem. She knew which role to play now, passive and motherly. It would soon pass.

He watched her as she heaped sugar into her cup. "I'm serious Isabelle. I'm very worried about the way that life is changing in the towns here."

"What do you mean, changing?" Isabelle asked, lighting a cigarette. The great crash of cymbals wasn't far off, she thought, then he'd calm down. He always got carried away with the mounting tension of the Karelia Suite.

"Society's beginning to break down. You can see it in the way strangers look at each other. It's an almost aggressive suspicion." He sighed. "Oh, there's always been a certain amount of it in the cities but now there's an anticipation of violence with the suspicion. What's worrying me is that the towns are picking up the cities' vibrations. You can feel it all around you. There's an increase in petty and violent crimes. There are more drunks and drug addiction. It's all getting closer to a breakdown of law and order. And then there are the religious and political extremists on their recruiting drives. They make things even worse."

"Oh, it's just a bad winter, Chris. It'll soon pass." She felt worried, he wasn't raving as usual, he was putting forward an argument, coolly and quietly, and she felt inadequate and unsure of what was expected from her.

"I don't think I can ever remember when there was such a clear division in society between rich and poor." He drank his coffee. "It's becoming the most awful mess. The economy is always going to be unstable and the monetary system in the West is bound to collapse eventually. We've got to accept that there will never be full employment again — that's a thing of the past. Throw in the colour problem and you've got all the makings of anarchy and civil war. If the anarchists aren't sure how to go about it there are plenty of terrorists around the world to show them how."

Isabelle felt lost, frightened and confused.

"What's all this to do with moving? Do you want to go to Bahrain?"

"Don't be so bloody stupid. What do you think is going on in the Middle East? Don't you read the papers? No — this is our home and if we want to keep the sort of life we're used to we're going to have to move out into the country."

Isabelle's wail rivalled Sibelius' cymbals and brought Mac out from under the sofa barking furiously.

"I don't want to move, Chris," she cried. "Where to? What about all our friends?"

"You'll find that all our friends would be only too pleased to come down to see you, that is if they've not already moved themselves."

He talked to her like a patient professor.

"But Chris," she pleaded desperately, "You know how much more expensive things are in the country, you've always said so and there's always the police to defend you in the town against violence..."

He shouted her into silence. "I'm talking about survival. I'm talking about the collapse of society. You talk about food prices, I'm talking about famine and growing your own food to live. You talk about the police defending you, I'm talking about the total breakdown of law and order. The police will be as hungry, rebellious and dangerous as anyone else."

He paused to turn off the record. Isabelle wiped her eyes on her apron and lifted the concerned Mac onto her lap. His halitosis, as he licked her face, acted on her like smelling salt, restoring her self control.

"Where do you want to move to?" she asked quietly.

He drew out an estate agents' circular from his file and handed it to her.

"This isn't a sudden decision." As he rubbed her shoulder his voice sounded tired. "I've been worried for the last two years, watching my England slowly change into a mean, apathetic society."

He stood in front of the fire, easing his temples with his fingertips and frowning with the effort of concentration. "I don't want to move any more than you do. I love it here, but Isabelle, I don't want to be like the Jews in Germany, leaving it until it's too late to get out, all because they hoped the problems would go away and wouldn't accept the reality of mass envy and hatred."

Isabelle looked at the circular, a smudgy picture showed the front of an old manor house. "Nodens".

She felt as if she was in the middle of a bad dream. "Imposing sixteenth century property," the circular read, "standing in two and a half acres, with extensive views of the moors and sea."

"Exmoor?" Isabelle exclaimed, looking at the map. She wondered whether Chris was having a breakdown or had in fact gone totally mad. Why hadn't he just moaned about the lack of sunshine, the need for a fruit diet or even become a Moslem, at least she could have followed him and adapted to his mood with the subservience of a well-trained ballroom dancer.

"It's actually Somerset." Chris had snapped back to life. "But you're near Exmoor forest. I've worked it all out, Isabelle."

He paced the room.

"Two and a half acres can keep you, Marcus and me easily. We'll have room to store coal and oil, there's plenty of wood, so we won't be affected by strikes. We'll keep chickens and grow all our own food. You're good in the garden."

"Not two and a half acres," she protested.

"We might even get our own water. I'll get more guns. We can easily see any approaching marauders.

He went on and on. Isabelle's mind kept wandering off into bizarre fantasies of Chris in a deer skin, Marcus shooting marauding Chelsea football supporters. Her back hurt and her head was throbbing and she wished, with all her heart, that Chris had never left Dubai.

"I couldn't possibly look after two and a half acres on my own."

"We're bound to find a local from Athairton. The village is only about three miles away."

He went into another tirade about the country and survival and as Isabelle watched him she wondered whether she could divorce him before he sold the house. She smiled to herself. She would be just like Daphne then.

"I'm glad you're happier about it all," Chris said, taking note of her smile, "I'm going to bed."

Watching the shadows flickering gently on the walls she felt like an aged Cinderella. She thought of her mother and an aching loneliness and yearning to be cuddled again swept through her.

As she scratched Mac's back and listened to his grateful grunts, she thought how strange it was that death could creep up and surprise you years later. She tried to remember her mother's face but the memory was blocked by the vivid recall of her death in the hospital. The sunken hollow that without its teeth hardly resembled a mouth.

She cleared away the coffee things and pushed the memory out of her mind.

His steady breathing gave the bedroom a strange feeling of alienation. Clutching Mac in her arms she watched him, fascinated that anyone could sleep with their arms folded in such a pompous position. Lowering the dog to the floor she crossed to the window and looked across the rooftops that were sparkling in the moonlight. The whole street slept under a blanket of snow. She felt as if she was the only person in the world who was awake.

The parked cars resembled a row of marrons glacés.

Something else was awake. She saw it huddled against one of the tyres.

The ginger tom looked up at her.

"I'm sorry," she whispered, willing her message to him.

In return, he shared with her his loneliness.

CHAPTER THREE

She had hoped that "Nodens" might have been sold or that after seeing a few friends and relaxing in Brighton Chris would forget the whole idea of moving. Bad weather made any thoughts of travelling impossible and as each night the television prophesied more sleet and snow Isabelle silently cheered.

Then on Tuesday, the thirtieth of January, it began to thaw and "Nodens" was still for sale.

Chris phoned his brother, David, who had a farm in Williton, a village near Taunton, to ask whether they could stay with them for a couple of days. David was thrilled. Visits were rare between the brothers.

Even Isabelle looked forward to seeing his wife, June, again. She was a bouncy blonde who during their years of marriage had changed the previously shy and retiring David into a confident, happy man with a warm sense of humour. Being the younger brother he had cheerfully accepted the role as Chris' subordinate. A gentle soul before his marriage, he had given Chris all the reverence that he had demanded, hanging on every word uttered as great pearls of wisdom.

June had altered all that.

On the day of David's wedding Chris, assuming the role of best man, in every sense of the word, had patronisingly placed his arm around his brother's shoulders and said, "You're a very lucky man, David."

"Yes," the blushing groom had replied.

June had immediately grabbed him by the arm and looking Chris directly in the eyes laughed, "Nonsense, I'm the lucky woman. David's the best fuck in England."

The journey was slow and tiring.

Because of the slush, many drivers were being sensible and

moved slowly. Some drove more slowly than others.

"Why do the slowest drivers have ears that stick out at the sides?" Chris fumed, honking at an old man who'd driven at twenty five miles an hour for the last twenty minutes.

Pulling out into the centre of the road, he dropped the Lagonda into third gear and after a terrifying skid finished, shaken but quite safe, back to front on a wide grass verge. The old man overtook him.

They arrived at the farm by four-thirty. The dusk was settling and Chris, having done a lap round the lanes to rival Stirling Moss, was cheerful again.

They were welcomed with homemade scones and tea around a roaring log fire. June was bursting with an unplanned, late pregnancy and in her bright orange woven smock, exuded maternalism.

"If it's not a boy this time, well too bloody bad." She laughed. "Honestly, Isabelle, I'd thought I was going to have a lovely time to myself now the girls are away at school. Then plonk."

The men sensing the inevitable nursery conversation, strode out of the lounge, theirs arms clasped around one another.

Isabelle sank back into the soft tweedy sofa. The warmth from the fire, the effects of the sweet tea and June's chatter made her drowsy. She glanced round the light modern room. A huge stone fireplace dominated the lounge. Brightly coloured curtains, bold modern paintings and an assortment of brilliantly coloured china and glass arranged in alcoves created a cheerful atmosphere. "Like being inside a bloody cuckoo clock," Chris had said.

"I know the exact moment it happened."

Isabelle looked at June's round, beaming face.

"It was when we were in Hammamet. The girls had gone to a disco and there was this marvellous sunset. You know Isabelle, I've always known the exact moment of each conception."

"Oh, I hope it's a boy." Isabelle purred with the memories of Marcus in a blue pram suit.

June had obviously started planning the dinner the moment that they'd phoned to say they were coming. In the centre of the polished pine table was a little bowl of snowdrops. "The first ones," she announced proudly.

There was homemade paté and roast local lamb with homegrown vegetables. Chris expounded on the effects of chemicals in foods and was gently reassured by David that their's were compost grown. Isabelle watched with amusement while Chris ate all the peas and beans. Of course they were frozen but the fact that they had been compost grown absolved them of any crime against his stomach.

She thought about the times when, to indulge his whim of only eating vegetables of the season, she had scoured Brighton, interrogating greengrocers over the authenticity of the vegetables' origins.

After large helpings of apple pie and cream, they relaxed with their coffee in front of the fire. Isabelle felt a great surge of love for June as she sat chubby and preening over the praises for her cooking. Then Chris, making quite sure he had their attention, repeated his reasons for wanting to move.

June was worried about how it would affect Isabelle, moving from a town to the quiet of the country.

David agreed with Chris. Several of his London friends had phoned wanting to know about property in Somerset. He agreed that it was only a matter of a year or two before the crunch, as he called it, came. No matter which government was in power.

"Of course life would be different, Isabelle," said June, "but you'd soon make friends and we're only about twenty miles away, aren't we David?"

"Yes," he replied. "I'd get some Alsatians though, if you're going to be away a lot, Chris."

Isabelle felt frightened. They were all assuming that they were definitely going to buy the house. "We might not like 'Nodens' when we see it," she said quickly.

The guest bedroom was directly above the kitchen. On the pine dressing table, were thoughtfully arranged bunches of tissues and cotton wool balls. A large china bowl of pot pourri scented the air.

Isabelle snuggled against the downy duvet and listened to the comforting sounds of another woman pottering in her kitchen last thing at night. She contemplated on their two different life styles and wondered whether she could settle in the country and remain as contented as June. Perhaps it would be possible at Carrington Farm but Chris hated modern houses. Isabelle shuddered at the memory of the smudged picture of "Nodens" on the estate agent's circular.

Chris turned over crossly, "Stop thinking, Bumble."

"How do you know I'm awake?" she whispered.

"You're making the bed rigid, go to sleep."

She heard David and June whispering as they came up the stairs. A passing car's headlights sent patterns across the ceiling. Isabelle drifted into an uneasy sleep.

"White rabbits."

June's cheerful voice and the sound of tea things chinking on a tray penetrated the heaviness of Isabelle's sleep.

"What?" she mumbled.

"First of February, first of the month, you say white rabbits for luck. Breakfast's downstairs, help yourself. I've got to nip down to the bank for David. I'll be back about ten." She bustled out.

Isabelle wondered whether she dared go back to sleep, then perhaps Chris would forget "Nodens". Instead, she drank some hot, sweet tea and by the time she'd got halfway through a cigarette she heard the sound of Chris' and David's voices. She was washed and dressed in five minutes flat.

On the road to Minehead they drove past cosy white-walled cottages. The sprinkling of snow on their thatched roofs reminded Isabelle of ornaments on a Christmas cake. The skyline was dominated by the undulating Quantocks that rose protectively around curling roads, streams and villages. Leaning back in the car and looking up to the summit Isabelle was aware of the red hue from the earth coming through the sea of snow-flecked bracken.

Chris drove on through more sleepy villages, past deserted local pottery and souvenir shops, isolated red sandstone churches and forbidding castles. All of them seemed to be waiting expectantly for the Easter tourist season.

Space, solitude and wilderness were Isabelle's first impressions of Exmoor.

Her sense of foreboding was increased by the strange blue haze that came from the earth, quite unlike the rich warmth of the Quantocks. The occasional proud house, dug into a hill, reminded her of the remoteness of the place. She felt like grabbing the wheel of the Lagonda and turning straight back for Sussex.

In the distance, across the rolling moors, the sea was grey and threatening.

A red deer appeared from behind a clump of pines and stared at them. The trees thickened as they turned off the main road and onto a narrow, winding one.

Quite suddenly they came upon Athairton.

The little village was silent. The only sign of life was the curling smoke coming from strange round chimneys, the smell of which, combined with the pungent farmyard manure, filled their nostrils as it seeped into the Lagonda. The first cottage had a board on the wall with an arrow painted on it, pointing to a shed at the back. "Arthur O'Leary Blacksmith" it said.

As the road curved into the main street a large oak sprouted from the centre of a small green. Beside it stood the "Tuatha Arms".

"What about a bite?" Chris suggested. "It's only about three miles from here and we're not meeting Mordant until two."

Sipping their beer in the oak-beamed bar were two old farmers who greeted them as they walked in. Chris gave his order to the pretty blonde barmaid with purple eyes who informed them that her name was Maeve.

As she cut the wholemeal bread and sliced the cheese she asked them whether they were on holiday and when Chris told her that they'd come to see "Nodens" she beamed at them.

"Oh, that's a lovely old house," she said. "We're all hoping that someone will buy it soon. It's not good for a house to be empty too long."

Isabelle was looking at a large bull's head that was hanging over the stone fireplace. "Is it always so quiet in the village?" she asked.

"Oh, no," said Maeve. "They're all getting ready for the party tonight. It's Bridget's birthday and everyone's bringing something. I'm in charge of the punch."

"What a friendly village," Chris observed. They sat round the pub fire, eating bread and cheese and sipping gin and tonics.

Maeve possessed that fresh open quality rarely found in town girls. She willingly told them all they wanted to know about the people in Athairton. They learnt that O'Leary, the smith was also the local plumber and Niall, of Niall's Stores was very clever with electricity. That there was someone called Old Karen who used to work up at "Nodens" before the previous owner, Mrs. Bourama, had "passed on". "And then there's Lugh."

Maeve paused while clearing their plates. "Well, Lugh can do almost everything."

"He's obviously the local bigwig." Chris said, when Maeve was out of earshot.

"I suppose everyone knows everything about each other here." Isabelle said.

"We'll probably find they all look alike," said Chris. "There's a lot of intermarriage in these small villages."

A mile past the village Chris turned the Lagonda right along a narrow lane. The car strained as it bumped along the uneven surface and stray tendrils from the hedges swiped at them as they passed by.

"We'd have to get a Landrover if we lived here," suggested Isabelle, knowing how much Chris loved his showy car. They slowed down for a small bridge under which a clear stream chattered its way down towards the sea. Then the road curled upwards for a mile, through a pine forest.

Mounted on stone pillars on either side of the iron gates stood two stone dogs. Their moss-covered eyes watched the approaching Lagonda.

Conifer trees lined the gravel driveway which led straight to a large oak doorway. Sitting in a red Ford Zephyr, parked in front of the old manor house, was Mr. Mordant, the estate agent, a small, dark, pock-faced man. He greeted them, then after stubbing his rolled cigarette into the gravel, took a large bunch of keys and unlocked the oak door.

As she stepped into the hallway, Isabelle was filled with a wonderful sensation of warmth and happiness.

The rational part of her brain reminded her that to live in this sprawling house with its heavy oak beams, large flagstone floors and strange corridors was complete and utter madness. It would be impossible to look after. Her emotions remained chaotic.

The bedrooms, some with sloping beams, others grand and stately with ornate marble washbasins, reminded her of childhood, when she'd played hide and seek in her parent's rambling home.

They entered a large, whitewashed kitchen, the focal point of which was a great blue Aga.

"Coke," the estate agent said. "Heats the whole house."

The windows overlooked an enormous vegetable garden. Isabelle could imagine the sounds of bees and the delicate scent of herbs that would drift through in the summer.

She experienced a strange warm sensation in her breasts and began to feel a growing, placid, cow-like tranquillity. As the two men moved out of the room she heard a sound similar to rushing waves in her ears.

Dizziness made her hold on to the window sill. A noisy heart beat thudded a fraction out of time with her own. Then a silence.

She breathed in deeply and resolved never again to drink gin at lunchtime.

"Isabelle, just look at this."

Chris was shouting from the lounge. She hurried to him. The view was magnificent. The tree-lined garden, with bowers, nooks and little corners, dropped in steps to lawns and orchards. On the bottom lawn was a summer house and from there the sweeping moors rolled softly down to the sea.

Mr. Mordant pointed to a dark cluster of trees about ten miles away. "Over by those trees, it dips into a valley. That's Culbone."

As Chris sauntered down to the lawns with Mr. Mordant, Isabelle explored nearer the house. A little pathway, overhung with willow and climbing roses, led to a walled garden. There, a wooden bench looked across a lily pond.

Isabelle wondered about Mrs. Bourama. Had she sat on the wooden bench in the summer and watched the May flies dance? She peered into the pond, looking for signs of goldfish. Nothing moved and the seat was too wet to sit on.

On the other side of the pond there was a gap in the stone wall. Ivy and creeper had grown across it. She pulled it away and found herself in a grotto. Over to the left stood a large greenhouse which contained an assortment of vines, climbing plants and plant pots.

She had the weirdest sensation of being watched. Looking upwards she was confronted by the gazing eyes of nine moss-covered stone heads. Two were repulsive, leering and grinning wickedly. The others, two of which were children's, were happy and smiling.

She laughed at herself. Her heart was thudding with fright and she felt thoroughly ashamed of her silliness. In the right hand corner, cut into the wall, was a small shrine. A wooden, madonna-like figure, looked upon her serenely. A gust of wind played whispering games with the trees. In the sky, a new moon was challenging the pale sun.

As she walked towards the orchards and lawns, the trees' whisperings pursued her. They grew louder arousing a host of forgotten memories. Childhood memories of exploring grasses that were too tall for her to see whether there were hidden spiders. She hadn't experienced those feelings since she'd been twelve. They'd stopped when she'd been sent to the convent.

She reached the summer house. Looking towards the sea, the wind crooned in her ears. She remembered hearing the same tunes when she was six and sitting on her father's shoulders, when he walked with her across the Sussex downs.

Looking towards Culbone, she was suddenly aware of a smell. A strange male smell. The same smell that had come from her father's tweed jacket. It seemed to be all around her. A rough, scratching sensation hurt her chin. As the smell grew stronger, pressure was exerted on her shoulders. "Chris," she screamed.

"We're here, Isabelle".

Her heart pounding, she ran back to the house, pausing briefly behind the kitchen wall to blow her nose and tidy her face. She didn't want to explain tearstained cheeks to Chris.

She felt safe again. The lovely, peaceful quiet of the lounge soothed away the terrors experienced on the lawns. "The roof needs a bit of work but otherwise the whole place seems to be remarkably sound." Chris was elated. It was four-thirty. Darkness was slowly encircling the house and Isabelle was dying for a cup of tea.

After Chris had assured Mr. Mordant that he would indeed be getting in touch with him about "Nodens" in the near future, they set off in the car. Driving down as far as the stone bridge was very tricky in the dark, the shadows deceiving Chris' eyes at every twist in the winding lane.

Despite his objections, she lit a cigarette, preferring a draught from the open window to shattered nerves.

As they passed through Athairton, they noticed that apart from a single lighted candle in each cottage window, the village was in darkness.

"Must be a power failure," observed Chris.

When they reached Carrington Farm they were cold and tired. June immediately ordered hot baths and supper by the fire. Isabelle felt grateful as the events of the day were washed away by June's bustling normality.

After the delicious steak and kidney pie, followed by fluffy cheesecake, Isabelle sank back into the comfortable armchair in a contented, sleepy stupor and listened to Chris describing "Nodens".

"Apart from the roof and odd repairs to the woodwork, it's in very sound condition."

He was flushed with port and extremely cheerful.

"It must be good air up there. The old girl was a hundred and two when she died."

Isabelle watched the flickering reflection of the fire on the coal-scuttle.

"There was a power cut in the village as we were driving through and there were little lighted candles in all the windows. It looked so pretty, it reminded me of an old Christmas card."

"I didn't think there'd been any power cuts around here," June remarked. She looked across at David. "They wouldn't be celebrating Candlemas, would they?"

"No," replied David, thoughtfully. "Candlemas is the second of February. Today's the first."

"What's Candlemas?"

"It's the custom of welcoming longer days," June explained. "'If Candlemas is fair and clear, there'll be two winters in the year'"

"I told you it was a power cut," Chris said.

"Well, pray for rain for us tomorrow," June went on, "Then we'll have a good harvest."

"What about our drive home?" Chris joked. "I'm not praying for rain."

"I wonder if it could have been Imbolc?" suggested David.

"Oh, no David, there's none of that around here." June laughed.

"What?" Isabelle asked quickly.

"David's just being stupid," June replied, "He's suggesting. . ."

"It's just an earlier festival for the same sort of thing," David cut her short, "Only they. . ."

"You mean. . ." June jumped in.

"I mean," he replied, "I mean the Celts" — he glared at his chubby wife — "celebrated a day earlier."

"With candles?" asked Isabelle.

"Well, more or less the same," he went on. "It was all tied up with the lactation of the ewes."

"We could move in tomorrow," Chris announced. "All we need is to start the heating system and get a carpenter. We could leave all the rest until we were living there."

"What do you think, Isabelle?" June asked gently.

"Well," she was hesitant, "I think we ought to think about it for a while."

Chris was irritated.

"We can't wait too long or the place will be snapped up. You've heard David say that other people are looking for property down here."

She felt tearful. She felt pushed into a situation and it frightened her.

"I just think we shouldn't rush into buying it," she said weakly.

"I'd like to get it all settled before I go back to Bahrain," Chris went on remorselessly.

"When's that?" David asked, aware of Isabelle's discomfort.

"Three weeks' time. I'd like to get things on the move before then, I've got some Athairton numbers, some fellows that are supposed to be good at their craft. You need locals who know the problems of the area."

Isabelle got out of the chair and helped June to clear the supper things to the kitchen.

She decided it was pointless to argue, Chris had obviously made up his mind. How was she to explain to him about the strange feelings that she had had about the place? Her intuition told her that if she moved into "Nodens" she would be in danger. Or was it danger that she feared? Or something else that she didn't quite understand?

As she dried the pans, June chattered on about various shops in Taunton that were good for materials and wallpaper. A memory flashed through her mind of Sister Mary Helen admonishing her. "Isabelle Cullen, you must learn acceptance." How weird, she thought. That whole area of her life had been forgotten until that very moment.

June put her arm around her. "Isabelle, I know how you feel. The trouble is, I know how Chris feels too, but if you really don't want to move, tell him, no."

Isabelle sighed, "That's the trouble June, I just don't know. I do like the house but. . ."

She looked at June's pale face and wondered whether to burden her with her strange fears, but decided not. June looked tired and drawn.

"Oh, I'm just being silly. It'll all turn out all right," she smiled.

Although fighting her tiredness and David's many requests to rest, June was finally taken off to bed by David, just after eleven. Chris followed soon after. He wanted to be up early to make some phone calls before leaving Carrington farm by ten o'clock.

Isabelle was wide awake, so she made some cocoa and settled down by the fireside to read some of the local country magazines.

Her attention was drawn to a sound in the fireplace. Tiny pockets of energy spluttered in the dying fire. A warmth crept up her spine. Hastily she turned to see whether she had dropped any ash down back of the chair.

The heat spread around her shoulders and through her hair.

A strange rushing sound pounded in her ears making her head

feel light. She tried to rise from the chair but her eyes wouldn't focus properly and her body felt heavy. The warmth moved down her arms. She felt herself drifting into what felt like a warm, enveloping sea.

Gasping, she shook her head and tried to free herself from a growing pressure around her waist. The warmth spread round her breasts. She could feel her breathing becoming more laboured. It grew hotter and hotter, almost as if she was drowning in a heated bath.

Quite suddenly it stopped.

She clambered out of the chair trembling violently.

She felt cold and wet.

Looking down the front of her nightdress, she saw with horror that her breasts were dripping milk.

CHAPTER FOUR

She ate her breakfast in a dazed silence, feeling isolated from the others and their morning activity.

David was arranging farm matters, June chattering to her daily help and Chris, with his usual indefatigable energy, had been up early, organised her with the packing, made a succession of phone calls and stopped only once, for a cup of coffee.

Her head reeled. She had hardly slept at all and when she had, there had been terrifying, searching dreams of running around "Nodens" gardens looking for something that she'd lost.

"Ready to go yet?" Chris beamed at her.

She willed herself together. As she walked to the kitchen cloakroom her body seemed detached from her head and her mind floated chaotically about.

They drove back towards Sussex, snow clouds following them. The potatoes that June had put in a plastic bag worked themselves loose and rolled about in the boot of the car. His voice was coming through a hollow pipe in her head.

"If all goes well, we can move one lot out in about ten days time, then I'll go down and see the carpenter chap and get the heating working."

She felt too weak to raise any objections as he arranged their future. The windscreen blurred and she drifted off to sleep. She awoke to the sound of the one o'clock news, crackling on the car radio. Looking out of the windows at the passing scenery, she recognised the soft Sussex landscape.

"You've made good time, Chris," she yawned.

He was pleased. "There's been hardly anything on the road going in this direction. This is what motoring ought to be like."

The newsreader announced more impending strikes and various experts interviewed talked solemnly about statistics and prophesied doom and gloom. As each pundit rambled on, Chris shouted his comments on the situation. "You see," he said turning to her, "I told you, it is coming. With any luck, we're going to be out just in time."

"It will be hard to sell Clifton Villas, with all this unrest, Chris."

He smirked. "No, that's where you're wrong. Everything's agreed. I should have it confirmed this evening."

Isabelle jerked against the seatbelt.

"Who?" she asked incredulously. "Who have you sold it to?"

"Yehedi," he replied smugly. "As I told you, the Arabs have got their troubles coming and he wants a place in England as a standby."

"You fixed all this up in Dubai, didn't you?

She felt like hitting him in his pink scrubbed ear.

"Well yes and no." He pulled up at a set of traffic lights and looked at her. "You see, I've been thinking about the way things were going for the past few years and one night Yehdi and I were having dinner and he told me about his fears for the future. He was very worried about the growing Moslem fanaticism. We agreed then that if I ever sold Clifton Villas and moved into the country, he would have first offer on it. You know how he loves Brighton. Don't you remember how he rushed around the Lanes when he came to stay?"

"Yes, I know he loves Brighton," she replied impatiently, "But why should he be safe in the town and not us? Why doesn't he want to move into the country?"

The lights changed and Chris drove on. "Isabelle, you must realise that the races in the Middle East think differently from us. They react collectively. The Chinese and the Japanese are the same. When the Arabs start it will be like setting light to a powder keg. Yehedi knows this, he's Westernised. I mean they won't charge about in gangs like the English. There'll be whole towns on the move, killing anyone in their way." He sighed, "Yehdi just wants a standby home, all ready for any emergency."

Isabelle groaned, "We're going to be really popular in Clifton Villas. They're going to really love a bunch of Arabs moving in."

Chris laughed. "Wogs in Cranford! What is the world coming to?"

Despite herself, she too saw the funny side of the arrangement. The Lagonda swerved erratically as they speculated on the effect that Yehedi, his wives, and innumerable children would have on the inhabitants of Clifton Villas.

They collected a very sullen Mac from Daphne who told them that the dog had pined and refused to eat for the two days that they'd been away. Clutching the cringing, sulking bundle of fur, Isabelle suggested that as they had a fresh chicken and vegetables from the farm, she might like to join them for dinner. Daphne happily accepted.

Pottering once more around her familiar kitchen "Nodens" seemed to her like a distant dream. As soon as they reached the house, Chris disappeared into the study to make more phone calls, leaving her to ponder on the strange experiences that had happened to her. She felt so normal now and the ridiculous happenings so far away that she wondered whether perhaps nitrates seeping into the water could have been the reason for her unusual physical sensations.

After preparing the vegetables and basting the chicken, she went up to bathe quickly before Daphne arrived, Mac scampering after her, determined not to let her out of his sight.

Luxuriating in sweetly scented bubbles, she wondered again about "Nodens". It did have a peaceful atmosphere. But then so did Clifton Villas.

A wave of sadness, a sense of impending loss, swept through her. Supposing Chris were wrong and England came through, as it always had. They would be stuck in the country and Clifton Villas would be lost for ever. She bravely stepped on to the scales, prepared for a gain in weight after June's cooking. She couldn't believe her eyes. Five pounds off. Eleven stone two. Perhaps the worry did it, she thought, as she powdered and slipped into a warm kaftan.

During dinner, Daphne enthused about the move. "Just think, Isabelle, you can come here and stay with me whenever you like and I'll come down to Athairton and see you in the country. It'll be lovely."

"We'll have a party before we go," said Chris, leaning back in the carving chair.

"I shall miss this room though, Isabelle. We've had some good times here, haven't we?"

"Mmm." She fought a wobbly mouth.

"Luckily all the furniture will fit perfectly into "Nodens". We could reproduce the atmosphere with this colour scheme, couldn't we? The ceilings will be lower but we can do some clever things with the paint to give an illusion of height, can't we?" he said, glancing around the room.

"I'd be only too glad to help," Daphne chimed in, aware of Isabelle's unhappiness. "Please can I help with the garden? I get so frustrated with my small patch in Kemptown."

Isabelle smiled at her. "Of course you can. I shall welcome it."

She thought of how Daphne would love the small garden by the lily pond. As she described it to her she found herself, despite her misgivings, infected by her friend's excitement. Later, when Chris had returned to the study, she confided in her about the dizziness and the strange sensation.

Daphne listened attentively.

"Oh, love, it's probably the change of life starting. It affects people in different ways, you know. Also the way Chris has sprung all this on you hasn't helped." She paused and looked at Isabelle. "Do you feel all right now?"

"Yes, I'm fine now."

She did feel well. It was surprising but the tiredness had completely gone.

Daphne went on, "It could have been something in the water. Perhaps you should warn June as she's pregnant."

Isabelle made a mental note to phone June first thing in the morning. She lit a cigarette and relaxed. Mac curled himself over her feet and Daphne entertained her with the latest gossip about a mutual friend.

She now understood why Chris had enjoyed his brief war. Given an impossible task to complete, he was happy.

Bribery with cash made sure that a removal van was available. People in Athairton, David, Mr. Mordant and Yehdi were all organised into preparation for D Day, or at least the first D Day.

Lower in the ranks, Isabelle had all the tedious jobs to do. The packing and other boring things. Chris would stand at the top of the stairs, issuing orders with apparent divine inspiration and she would charge into battle. It was all planned. Half the house would be ready to be moved by the thirteenth of February. Chris was going to see to it all.

He would go with the men to "Nodens" and get all the work started there while Isabelle remined behind, running things until he returned. All the arrangements were altered when Yehdi phoned him on the twelfth.

"I've got to fly to Bahrain right away." He was furious about his thwarted plans.

"Now, look, I've written it all down. The removal men are coming at eight o'clock. They should be ready to leave by ten. You're to drive straight down to meet Mordant at "Nodens" at two-thirty. David's arranged a delivery of coke and managed, through a friend of his, to get the phone connected. This man Nialls will be there with Mordant. He'll check out the Aga, the wiring and make sure the heating is working. The removal man should be there by four at the latest. This envelope is for Nialls, this one for the removal men and don't give it to them until they've finished their work. When all that's completed, David and June are expecting you to stay with them. Give David these envelopes. They're for the coke and the post office engineer."

He continued as Isabelle checked his shirts and clean pants for the trip.

"The following day, that's the fourteenth, be back at the house by ten o'clock. Lugh the carpenter will be waiting to start work on those sills. He'll be there all day. O'Leary will arrive about midday to check the plumbing and drains. Oh, and I should get in touch with this Karen woman."

"Who?" she asked, on her knees in the wardrobe, looking for his sandals.

"The woman the barmaid told us had cleaned for the old lady."

She found the sandals and stuffed them into his case. "Yes," she shouted, dashing to the bathroom for his sponge bag. She grabbed a bottle of 4711 and threw it in, remembering how it cooled him when he couldn't sleep at night. He was catching a helicopter to take him from Gatwick to Heathrow. Isabelle drove him to Gatwick, trying to concentrate on the road and absorb all his last minute orders at the same time.

"Arrange a party for the middle of March and ask Marcus' housemaster if he can have the weekend free."

"Half term starts in four days' time," said Isabelle, staring hard at the cat's eyes.

"Oh, you'll be back in time," Chris replied, "I'll phone you from Bahrain to let you know when I'll be home."

"Yes."

The drive back was wonderfully calm and at a steady 45 miles an hour. Emerging through the little clouds of fog around Pease Pottage she could see the dark shape of the Downs on the skyline. Climbing cars' headlights moved across them, like flashing sequins on a black velvet dress.

Walking up the steps to her front door, she could smell the burning wood from her lounge fire. Pausing in the porch, she looked down the silent street and breathed in the crisp night air. The sky was clear, pierced only by the spire of the Catholic church and the slow-moving lights of an overhead plane.

The seagulls that usually clucked at night before a weather change were silent.

"A good sign," Isabelle thought out loud. "With any luck it will be a clear run tomorrow."

Mac hovered round her as she packed an overnight bag. She'd phoned Daphne and asked her to keep an eye on the Aga. Now all she had to do was to make sure that she woke up at six-thirty. She set two alarm clocks and placed a call with the telephone operator. She needn't nave bothered. The ginger tom fought a Siamese at six o'clock and Mac's barking completed the reveille.

Snow was forecast on the seven o'clock news. The removal men, contrary to Chris's timetable, didn't arrive until eight-twenty.

Mac started screaming as soon as he saw her loading the car, so she bunged him unceremoniously, with his dog bowl and minced morsels, into the front seat.

The men left at ten-fifteen and after scribbling a note for Daphne, Isabelle followed at ten-thirty. The sky was clear with a pale lukewarm sun. She overtook the removal van on the Shoreham roundabout and speeded up trying to increase the gap between them, in order to catch up on Chris's schedule. Mac popped up a couple of times from under the seat, but lost his confusion when the heater was turned on and curled up into a contented ball.

She was apprehensive. Chris was so organised. How in God's name was she going to manage in his place? She was bound to fail him. Hadn't she always? Every important dinner party during their early married life had been a nightmare for her. She had always said the wrong things to the wrong person. Still, she thought, he should have been warned from their period of engagement.

Attending an important legal dinner in London as his tulle-covered fiancee she'd become entangled in her evening gloves. She'd watched the older women carefully unbutton theirs and fold them back and tried to do the same. She'd ended up with soggy nylon fingers, flicking soup over the High Court Judge on her right.

A smattering of sleet across the windscreen pulled her out of her masochistic reverie. As she continued to drive further west it grew colder and grey clouds hung heavily in the sky, confirming the earlier weather report on the news. She reached Athairton by two-thirty. Turning off into the lane leading to "Nodens" she had an overwhelming urge to pee. Not wanting to be the lone tinkler at "Nodens", reverberating to strangers' ears, she pulled up at the nearest clump of trees.

As an icy wind blasted her bare bottom, she thought how unfair it was that men could pee with hardly any alteration to their clothing.

Mac joined her in the primitive ritual, yapping excitedly, and by the time she had shoved him back into the car, she was late for Mr. Mordant. His red Ford was parked outside the house. Next to it stood a small white van with "Nialls Stores" written on the side. Calling Mac and clutching her bags and baskets she was let into the hall by Mr. Mordant who, after relieving her of the heaviest basket, assured her that everything was under control. "I've done everything your husband wanted. Is he not with you?"

"He's had to go to Bahrain," Isabelle tried to sound confident. "So I'll deal with everything."

"In that case I'll introduce you to Mr. Nialls. He's in the kitchen at the moment." He led the way to the kitchen. "Oh, and these are all the keys," he added. "They've got labels on them, so you'll know where they belong."

Mr. Nialls looked just as a village storekeeper should. He was a round, red-haired, jovial little man with a spiky red beard. "Hello, Mrs. Carrington, did you have a pleasant journey?"

Isabelle liked him at once. "Yes, thank you, she replied.

"I met your brother-in-law, Mr. Carrington."

"Oh, good," Isabelle felt her smile growing wider in the effort to complement Mr. Nialls'. His blue eyes twinkled and his rosy cheeks shone, so that he resembled a friendly garden gnome.

"It's nearly caught," he said, indicating the Aga. "It'll take about an hour and then this whole house should start warming up again." He wiped the top of the Aga lovingly as if it were his own bacon shelf.

"Your brother-in-law, he's a real goer, isn't he? Still it helps to know someone at the exchange."

"Pardon?", she enquired.

"You've got your phone connected, didn't ye know?" He looked at her in surprise. "Sometimes it takes months around here."

"Ah, yes, marvellous," she said. "We've been very lucky."

"It's a good omen," he added, "Dis Pater is smiling on you."

"Mmm," Isabelle smiled, preoccupied with filling Mac's bowl with water and placing it on the floor.

"He's arranged the coke too, I'll show you." He led her through the scullery and out of the back door. "That shed there. That's where the coke is." He pointed to a group of black wooden sheds near the garden wall. 'And next to it is your coal shed. It's got a bit left over from Mrs Bourama. Your brother-in-law's left about a ton of coke in that shed. Came with one of his workers, he did this morning. O'Leary told me. He came up with him to turn the water on and everything. He'll be back tomorrow, by the way.'

"Yes, yes I'm expecting him." She was relieved. So far everything was going as planned.

Mr. Mordant was hovering in the doorway, clutching his coat tightly and shivering. "If you don't need me any more, Mrs.

Carrington, I'll be off. I've left my card by the phone, if you have any queries."

"Thank you, Mr. Mordant."

"The keys are all in the kitchen," he said, edging back into the house. "There are two back door ones, but they're clearly marked."

"Thank you," she said. "My husband will probably be in touch with you very soon."

"I hope you'll be happy here," he said, moving to the front door.

"I'm sure we will be."

He climbed awkwardly into his car. "Well, I'll be saying goodbye."

"Goodbye," she echoed, waving gently like the Queen Mum.

Mr. Nialls watched her as she unpacked her teapot and kitchen cups. The least she could do, she explained, was to make sure that the removal men had some tea when they arrived. "There's some soup in that flask if you'd like some," he offered.

Isabelle accepted gratefully.

"My wife made it. She's handy with soups, I'll say that for her."

The tubes leading to Isabelle's stomach clutched at the warm soup gratefully. A warm glow spread through her veins, just as the heat began to throb through the water system. Clunks and rattles echoed through the house in sympathy with her relaxing body.

Mr. Nialls wandered about the house checking the places for new points to be fitted, gossiping as he went, about the people in the village. She suddenly remembered about the old cleaner suggested by the barmaid.

"Is the old lady called Karen on the telephone?" she enquired.

"Oh, no, she hasn't a phone. No need, ye see, she's right in the village. Hazel Cottage, that's hers."

"I was hoping that she might be interested in helping here."

"I should think she'd be only too pleased," he said, scratching his head. "Would you be wanting Sam Powell as well?"

"Who's he?"

"He used to keep Mrs. Bourama's garden for her. See those conifers?" he said, pointing through the bedroom window to the trees lining the driveway below. "He planted all those, Sam did.

41

Talks to all the vegetables, you know," he said seriously. "Every year, "Nodens" took prizes for the vegetables." Isabelle thought of Chris and his obsession about home-grown vegetables, and beamed at Mr. Nialls.

"I'd be so grateful if you would," she replied, thanking providence for the unexpected bonus. Looking out of the window again, she noticed dark clouds gathering in the south-west. Shivering, she returned to the kitchen where it was warmer. She lifted the Aga cover. The plates were beginning to heat up. Soon they'd be hot enough to make tea.

Rolling up her sleeves and putting on her overall she set about cleaning the old fashioned sink with its slatted wooden draining board. Next to be scrubbed was the big larder with its stone walls and cool marble shelves. By four o'clock, with a sparkling clean larder and the smell of disinfectant everywhere, she put the large heavy kettle that she'd brought with her on to the now hot Aga plate and prepared for the arrival of the removal men.

Mr. Nialls, having finished his work, switched on the kitchen light. The sudden brightness in the kitchen brought her attention to the growing darkness. Outside, snow was beginning to fall gently. "Will you be all right now?" he asked with concern. "Only I promised to be home by four, you see."

"Yes, I'll be fine, thank you Mr. Nialls," she replied, feeling less confident than she sounded. "They should arrive any moment now."

As she watched his van drive away, she noticed the snowfall beginning to quicken. Big fat snowflakes settled on the bushes like quivering butterflies. She thought that she'd better phone David as it was by now four thirty. June answered the phone. She was just giving an account of her progress and situation at that moment when she heard the sound of the approaching van.

Promising June to hurry over to them as soon as possible, she rang off. The men were apprehensive because of the worsening weather. They unloaded hastily declining Isabelle's offer of tea. By six o'clock they had finished and after collecting their envelope, hurriedly departed.

As she watched the tail lights of the van disappear the south westerly wind began to moan round the house.

The snow was gathering into small drifts. Shutting the heavy oak door quickly she turned and looked at the tea chests dumped all over the hall and decided that she would leave the unpacking until the following day.

It was as she went to lock the back door that she realised that Mac was missing.

"Mac," she shouted. She listened intently for a whine or the tinkle of his address disc as he scampered along to her.

Silence.

She ran down the corridors, switching on the lights and looking into all the rooms. There was no sign of the dog.

Her whistling couldn't compete with the noise of the wind. It shrieked across the garden, whipping the bushes and trees into dancing, grotesque shapes. He was not in any cupboard or behind any door. She searched for all the warm pipes that he might have curled up against. "He must be outside," she ranted to herself. "Stupid bloody mut."

As she opened the back door, the wind pushed past her and rushed down the corridor, slamming doors and rattling windows.

"Machiavelleeee," she yelled.

She heard a small whimper. She could hardly see through the swirling snow. It stung her face and as she shouted, her mouth was invaded by suicidal snowflakes. He was in the coke shed, shaking with fright and looking like a black demon.

Yanking him out, she slammed the shed door shut and fled back to the kitchen, where he danced around, barking happily and leaving sooty paw marks all over the clean floor. "You bad dog," she grumbled, as he followed her round all the rooms where she switched off all the lights.

The large lock was stiff.

Mac clung to her legs, the snow blowing through his whiskers, as she tried to turn the key. At last it clicked and picking up her bags and the dog bowl, she tucked the protesting dog under her arm and fought her way to the car.

It just wouldn't move. The wind had blown against the front wheels, creating a small drift. As the Lagonda heaved against it, the snow packed itself more firmly into the wheels. Fear flooded through her veins, making her dizzy with panic. What would

Chris do, she thought frantically. The answer floated up through the depths of her subconscious. Dig!

Leaving Mac inside and the engine running, she trudged to the front of the car. As she kicked and pushed the snow with her flailing arms the wind stung her eyes, forcing hot tears of rage at her helplessness. Shivering, she climbed back into the car and eased the gear into first. A slight movement forward raised her hopes, then the wheels were spinning. The engine roared as she panicked and pressed the accelerator flat down.

It was no use. She was stranded.

Collecting her bags she returned to the house, leaving the dog inside the car, screeching with fright. "You wait," she shouted at the Cairn. "It's all your fault, you little fiend."

At least it was warm in the house, she thought, as she dumped her bags. Returning to the car, she could see the dog looking pitifully through the window. She thought that his black face framed by the snow covered glass would have made a perfect Christmas card for the Battersea Dogs Home.

He clung to her like a naughty child as she fought the wind, her numb fingers clutching his dog bowl. After locking the heavy oak door, she went to telephone David. June answered the phone, anxiously.

"Isabelle," she cried. "I was just going to ring you. It's terrible here. There's huge drifts. . ."

David took the phone away from her. "Look Isabelle, if you'll be all right there, stay put. The roads are terrible." She felt abandoned.

"Is there no chance of you getting here?" she asked tremulously. The line began to crackle. "It's happened so quickly," he shouted, "We're almost cut off from Williton. It would be madness to try and get across in the dark."

Sensing her worry, he asked her, "Have you any food there?"

"I've got some tea and biscuits and a Mars bar," she joked weakly.

"Did you bring any bedding?"

She pulled herself together. "Yes, it's all right. I brought the spare beds down and all the summer linen and I've got plenty of blankets here, so don't worry." As she talked she became calmer.

"And the heating is working?"

"Yes, I'll be fine David, don't worry."

"Well, phone me if you're worried about anything."

"I will."

"I'll get to you as soon as I can. Okay?"

"Okay." She replaced the receiver. As she put the kettle on to make tea, she wondered how the removal men had fared. To be stranded on the moors could be fatal. She remembered newspaper stories of people suffocating while trying to keep warm in their stranded cars, by leaving on their heaters. She shuddered.

It was only three miles to Athairton. She wondered whether she could walk there. Outside the snow fell relentlessly, the gusts of wind throwing it around into a carnival of icy Catherine wheels. She decided not to try.

She chose the small spare bedroom overlooking the drive and facing Culbone. It had a large centrally heated radiator and the windows were in reasonably good repair. As she carried the blankets and linen to the bedroom her footsteps echoed on the bare wooden floors of the corridors. Mac's padding steps and clicking nails followed her and eased the feeling of isolation a little, but she wished that she had a radio with her so that she could drown the noise of the wind.

The sound of running water for her bath was a lovely familiar one. It took away the eeriness of the howling wind. Surrounded by her soap, toothpaste and other familiar toiletries the situation became more normal. Mac sat by happily, listening to her singing.

The wind chased up the overflow pipe, hitting a jarring musical note that halted her warbling. Cold air rushed in, pulling goose pimples from her arms.

She fought the noise by pulling out the plug and releasing the water against the offending elements.

Luckily an electric fire had been packed amongst some of Marcus' old toys. Mr. Nialls's new electric point was tested and it worked.

Books, a rug, the painting of Cow and Cow Parsley and a lighted candle in a silver candlestick created an atmosphere of homely warmth.

As she sat smoking and drinking tea in her bed, her blue fluffy dresing gown wrapped snugly around her, she heard the wind die down although the snow continued to fall steadily. She wished that she could have had someone with her to share the spectacular view. It was like a child's vision of fairyland. Memories drifted back of being with her father at a pantomime and seeing the dance of the silver fairies in the land of the icicles.

Mac was curled up on the bed, warming his back against the heat of her legs. Drowsiness overcame her and a sensation of floating.

Down at the end of the dark tunnel of sleep, was a pinprick of light.

As she floated towards it, it grew larger, filling her vision with brightness. She wasn't sure that she wanted to go. It was much easier to float back down the tunnel into the darkness. Someone was with her, holding her. She could hear the second heartbeat and feel the breathing in her ear. A warmth moved through her, then strong hands pulled her detached hot mind through the light and she was free.

She soared into bright blue skies like a bird and then dropped quite suddenly into a field. She felt anxious, as if someone was waiting for her and she was late.

She could see all around her, as if she were an all-seeing eye.

Grass waved and birds flying past glanced in her direction.

She seemed to be sitting on a fence.

Was she one of the birds?

Cows chewed their cud and stared at her.

There she was. The waiting one.

A child, sitting in the grass, intent on making a daisy chain.

Who was she?

She was about nine. Her little brown shoulders gleamed through the straps of her sunsuit as she split the stalks and pushed the flowers through to make the chain. Her little fair-haired head, bowed in concentration, suddenly jerked up, as if aware of her presence.

Her head began to turn towards her, when she felt herself being pulled away.

She didn't want to go. She wanted to see the child's face.

Her head started to thump. Colours poured into her vision until she was drowning in a sea of liquid rainbow. Her ears pounded and she was sweating.

Was she dying?

Her heart thumped louder.

"Mrs. Carrington?"

She struggled out of coloured mud. A sound of barking.

"Mac, what's the matter?" she murmured.

It was a white, daylight world and she was alive in "Nodens". There was a thumping on the front door.

"Mrs. Carrington?"

Struggling to the window she looked down.

The only disturbances in the soft white landscape were sleigh tracks and footprints to the door. The Lagonda resembled an elongated igloo. The knocking started again.

Isabelle looked at her watch. It was eight o'clock. Smoothing down her rumpled dressing gown she ran to open the door. His appearance against the snow covered background was one of darkness. As her eyes focused to absorb detail she saw his blue eyes twinkling at her and a gentle, humourous mouth smiled to reveal even, creamy teeth.

"I'm Lugh," he said.

"Oh," she said, flushing, aware of her crumpled dressing gown. "How do you do."

Strapped to his sledge was a carpenter's bag and a few planks of wood. A covered basket rested on the top. The snow's reflection lit up his weatherbeaten face as he turned to untie the straps. "We saw that your car didn't come back down through the village last night," he said in his soft Somerset burr. "The women got together and I think you'll find all the food you need for now."

He carried the basket through the door and into the kitchen. There was freshly baked bread, a jar of damson jam, patted butter, a little bowl of cream cheese, half a dozen eggs, a jar of coffee, fresh milk in a screw top bottle, a homemade pork pie and a bone with a label attached. "For the dog" was printed on it. Isabelle was quite overwhelmed by the villagers' kindness.

"We couldn't get up to you last night but Nialls said you'd be warm enough. We watched the van go past, though how far they got we don't know." He paused, then picked up the bucket. "I'll go and get some more coke for you, shall I?"

She was suddenly overcome by shyness and could only nod, gratefully. She watched him walk towards the coke shed until the smell of the bread brought her attention back to the food and the realisation that she was ravenous.

Dressed, her appetite satisfied, she sat in Marcus' old nursery chair by the Aga, relishing her cup of coffee and smoking her first cigarette of the day. The sound of Lugh's hammering drifted downstairs from the bedrooms. Mac gnawed his bone happily and the contented warmth that she had felt when she had first stepped over the threshold two weeks ago returned again.

David phoned to see that she was all right. He and June had been snowed in and had to dig their way out from the front door. Apparently, all over the country people had been reported stranded in cars or cut off from reach in their villages.

She found herself warming towards Lugh as they shared their lunch. With his amusing stories about the village and his simple approach to life she felt confident enough to relate her dream to him. He listened thoughtfully and then smiled.

"The temple of healing," he said gently.

"I beg your pardon?"

"Nuadha, the temple of healing." He gazed at her and she felt a flush creeping up her neck and into her cheeks.

"Nuadha?" she asked.

"Nuadha or Nodens, the temple of healing. The healing would take place during sleep."

"So that's the meaning of Nodens?"

"Yes."

She was fascinated. "Where does the word come from?"

"It's Celtic," he said, getting up from his sitting position on the tea-chest. "Carrington? Mmm. . . What was your maiden name?" he asked.

"Cullen," she replied.

"Ah," he laughed. "You belong."

He was right, she did feel as if she belonged.

She watched as he walked back towards the stairs and noticed that without his lumberjacket he was a slim, athletic man of about thirty six. It was strange, she thought, but he seemed to radiate energy and warmth.

Bright-eyed and feeling fighting fit, she scrubbed down the airing cupboard, attacked the bathrooms, measured up for curtains and shifted the furniture around. By four o'clock the light was fading and she longed for a cup of tea. As she listened to the kettle hissing she remembered Nialls telling her about the coal in the other shed. Throwing on her coat and grabbing a cardboard box she made her way towards it.

The snow spilt into her Morlands and her hands became quite numb but she managed to hump a load of coal back to the kitchen. Her fingers were hurting with the cold and pains shot up her arms. She held her hands under the running tap for a while, but they still ached. Drying them with a towel helped a little but then she saw Lugh's great pair of lined gloves on the mantel-piece. She put them on and clasped them tightly together. Pins and needles tingled through her hands, returning them to normality.

A warm smell came from the gloves and an intense heat rushed through her body.

In her inner ear echoed the strange sounds of waves pulling at a beach. Her breasts and womb were on fire. The male smell that she had experienced by the summer house was all around her. Some incredible force held her in a sea of sensations. Her hearing was so acute that she could hear the kitchen walls breathing.

As she drifted dreamily into the hall, the sounds of singing and laughing floated into her consciousness. Then she saw the lights bobbing outside the window.

"Mrs. Carrington?"

Reality came back as Lugh switched on the light and walked down the stairs. "Are you all right?" he asked.

Before she could reply, there was a loud knocking on the door. Outside, she was greeted by a crowd of smiling, chattering people. In their assorted coloured hats they resembled a gathering of pixies.

Seated on a large sledge behind them was an old lady, clutching a wicker washing-basket. Mr. Nialls pushed himself forward, laughing. "Mrs. Carrington, we've brought you a "Wellcome to Nodens" party."

"Oh," she gasped. "Oh, Mr. Nialls, come in, do come in."

"It's a bit late in the year for wassailing, isn't it?" shouted Lugh. They all shrieked with laughter, then after stamping their boots to get rid of the snow they dribbled into the hall, one by one. "Mrs. Carrington, this is my wife Olwyn." Mr. Nialls ushered forward a smiling, round-faced country woman whose rosy cheeks matched his own.

"How do you do." Isabelle went to shake hands then realised that she was still wearing the large gloves.

"Oh, Lugh," she cried, "I've got your gloves on. I borrowed them. I hope you don't mind."

There was a hush as they all turned to Lugh. His eyes twinkled and the corners of his mouth twitched with amusement.

"Mrs. Carrington," he laughed, "Will you do me the honour of accepting them as a present, a moving-in present?"

The men all laughed with him. The old lady, who had been sitting on the sledge, came forward, her eyes gleaming.

"Will you accept his handsome present?"

Isabelle felt ridiculously giggly.

"Yes, of course I'll accept."

They all cheered.

"Oh," she gasped. "The kettle." She rushed into the kitchen, to see the kettle spouting like a jet engine.

They all followed her in. The basket was placed in the centre of the floor and the cover whipped off to reveal a feast. As they unpacked all the food and drink, they introduced themselves. It turned out that the old lady was "Old Karen".

Isabelle told her how glad she was to meet her and then went on to explain, feeling slightly embarrassed, how she'd brought the coal in and made her hands cold and really only borrowed the gloves. The old lady hugged her, comfortingly, "Never mind, dear," she said, "I'm sure he would have given them to you in any case."

Being sorrounded by so much warmth and spontaneous friendship was too much for Isabelle and she felt embarrassing tears of happiness prick at her eyelids. "Oh, how kind you all are to visit me like this," she blurted.

Lugh saved the moment by picking up the coal and carrying it into the lounge. "I've got some shavings of wood upstairs, Arthur, will you get them?" Before he did as Lugh had asked, Arthur introduced himself to Isabelle.

"I'm O'Leary," the large, good natured looking man boomed, "And this is my wife, Gwynneth." He brought forward a slim, high cheeked woman with a strong friendly face. "I'll be right there Lugh," he shouted as Gwynneth welcomed Isabelle to a happy life at "Nodens."

A tall, blond, good looking young man with a kind, open face and a young woman, also tall with long, blonde hair and a face full of friendly freckles, introduced themselves as Dermot and Granya. "Mrs. Carrington, we've brought a record player in case you don't have one, so we could have music, do you mind?"

Isabelle could have hugged them. "It's the one thing I've really missed, being here on my own. Oh yes, let's have some music," she said, feeling slightly mad.

A grey-haired old man gave her a cup of apple wine and a cheese straw. "Mrs. Carrington, I'm Sam Powell," he said. "I used to look after the garden here."

Isabelle sipped her wine. It was delicious. "It's apple champagne, I made it," he informed her proudly. "From the apple crop here, last year. The old Apple Tree Man was good to "Nodens" last year."

Isabelle loved Old Sam immediately. He talked about the garden as if it was a nursery full of his own children. He told her he wasn't sure if it was the right thing to do but he had kept his eye on the garden.

"I didn't want it to feel forgotten, you see," he said solemnly. "Now I'm working here, officially like again, I'll get the onions sown as soon as possible. As soon as the cats are on the prowl."

"It'll be a good July and September but a very unsteady August." The voice came from a middle-aged woman, busily warming food at the Aga. She introduced herself as Sybil.

"Bridget told me. She also says the crops will be late this year." She nodded knowingly at Sam.

A catchy, country jig echoed through the house accompanied

by the happy laughter from the villagers gathered round the fire. Isabelle sat on a cushion in the middle. She felt dizzy with all the warmth and comradeship.

The food was spiced with country herbs and the conversation buzzed amongst them like the sound of merry bees. "Don't forget to save your soot for the garden now," Sam reminded her, "And next month, before the full moon, we'll get the peas and beans in."

Arthur O'Leary got up and told some funny rhymes, which were obviously well known to the others as they joined in with every last line and shouted with laughter. Isabelle felt her cheeks aching with giggling. "For my next one, it's a bit naughty though, would ye be offended Mrs. Carrington?"

"No, no," she shouted wildly.

He stood in the centre of the floor, his hands behind his back and looked at them all sternly which immediately brought yells of laughter.

"'Behave yourself nicely,' said father
'For manners have long been our boast.'
'Manners be buggered,' said Charlie,
And did a gert gob on his toast."

Isabelle felt hysterical. The others, incited by her appreciation, urged each other on to entertain her.

"Do you know what the first sign of madness is?" asked Mr. Nialls.

"No," replied Isabelle.

"Hairs on the palms of your hands."

"And do you know what the second is?"

"No."

"Looking for them!" he shouted with glee.

Full of good food and mellow with the apple champagne they listened while Granya sang a poignant folk song about love and sadness.

Isabelle caught Lugh staring at her and felt herself blushing. Life felt so complete for her at that moment that Brighton seemed a million light years away. When had she ever relaxed so easily with a group of comparative strangers?

She felt no fear, just a sense of belonging, as if she had returned to a large family. The air felt warmer as she let them all out of the front door. Loving arms hugged her as they said their farewells.

"The trees are on the drip," Sam shouted as he made his way down the drive. "The snow'll be clearing tomorrow."

Lugh was the last to leave.

"You'll be going back to Brighton tomorrow, I suppose."

"If the snow melts, yes." she replied.

"Old Karen'll let me in, so I'll leave all my tools here. I'll have it all finished by the time you get back." He shook her hand. "It's been a pleasure meeting you, Mrs. Carrington."

"Won't you need your gloves for the cold?" she asked.

He looked at her curiously. "Oh, no, I gave them to you as a present. I want you to keep them. Besides," he smiled mysteriously, "It's after midnight, I can't take them back now."

She watched him drag the sledge along the snow covered drive. As he reached the front gates, he turned and waved and she waved back. Something about the way he had waved stirred a memory. It fought its way through the locked compartments of her subconscious and hovered, not sure of its truth.

As he closed the gates behind him he shouted, "I'll see you at Easter."

Tears sprang to her eyes and a smell of tweed overwhelmed her. The memory, sure of itself, surged relentlessly into her consciousness.

He had waved like that. He had turned and shouted, "See you at Easter," in 1943, at the gates of the convent.

He didn't return at Easter. She never saw him again.

His squadron had all been shot down, over the English Channel.

"Daddy," she whispered. . .

CHAPTER FIVE

She slept heavily, like an exhausted child after a traumatic birthday party. The strange dream returned with the unseen helper, guiding her again to the same field, where the little girl sat patiently waiting for her. This time, when the child began to turn to her, her view was obstructed by a herd of cows, pushing into her line of vision and hiding the small face from her.

She had returned down the long dark tunnel into a deep untroubled sleep, waking the next morning feeling refreshed and exhilarated.

The snow-covered landscape sparkled in the bright sunlight. As Sam had predicted, the dripping from the trees had melted the snow, so that green patches had appeared on the lawns, and on the driveway the gravel and tarmac had emerged as if by magic. David telephoned her at nine o'clock and advised her not to try and reach them at Carrington Farm, as all the small lanes from Williton were blocked by abandoned cars.

"I'd get straight back to Brighton, if I were you, Isabelle. I think there's going to be more snow later."

"What about these envelopes?" she asked him.

"Oh, leave them at Smith's garage. I'll pick them up from there."

O'Leary's truck drew up outside the house just before she left and Old Karen scrambled out, wrapped up in layers of knitted shawls like a small homemade tea cosy.

"Morning Mrs. Carrington," shouted O'Leary. "That was a good party last night, wasn't it?" His round face beamed at her.

Before she could reply Old Karen jumped in. "We all ended up throwing snowballs at each other. Like mad kids we were." She slapped her skirts and cackled wickedly. "We got Lugh by surprise, didn't we? Caught him at the bridge."

She stared at Isabelle's bags. "Oh, of course, you're off to get your son now, aren't you. Half term, isn't it?" "Yes," Isabelle smiled at the moving tea cosy. "He breaks up tomorrow."

Old Karen looked at her solemnly. "Well, you'd better set off straight away, in case you get caught in more snow. Don't worry, we'll look after "Nodens" for you."

Isabelle looked at her warm country face and wanted to hug her. The old woman, sensing her inhibition, reached out and squeezed her by the arm.

"You hurry back to us now," she said. "We'll be missing you."

"Yes," echoed O'Leary. "Hurry back, the house is just beginning to look happy again." She assured them that she would and drove off quickly.

The sound of well-modulated vowels bounced off the Gothic stone walls and assaulted her ears as she approached the quadrangle from the car park. Tired, self-sacrificing masters wandered among groups of parents, nodding, listening and occasionally withdrawing discreetly from a sudden burst of unexpected halitosis.

Watching the various greetings between parents and sons she wondered why so many public school parents treated their children so politely. They touched them carefully and at a distance, as if they were small sugar lumps attached to sticky silver tongs.

Chris's parents were like that. His mother's greatest show of affection was an inclined, powdered cheek. Her security was founded on prejudice and her great talent the spreading of negative despondency. His father, on the other hand, was quite the opposite. He showed affection with hearty punches and thwacks on the back. His philosophy was based on the premise that if it moved you killed it and if it was still you drank it. His greatest talent was inspired arrogance.

With a wide grin and gangly arms Marcus walked towards her. His wrists and ankles stuck out at the ends of his jacket and trousers, and puberty-stricken pimples peeped out from under his fringed hair. Hugging him passionately in the company of so much restraint made her feel like an abandoned gypsy at a Quaker meeting.

During the drive home they planned their week-end itinerary, with Marcus insisting on plenty of steaks and "slobbing about". Appealing to her for sympathy he described his fifteen-mile hike with the school cadet corps. "In the snow?" Isabelle asked with horror. Marcus piled on the agony until as usual his imagination overtook the bounds of plausibility.

Later that evening, while Marcus shovelled down steaks and chips and Mac growled with jealousy, she explained about the move.

"That's three from our house," he said.

"How do you mean?"

"Well, Nicky's and Tom's parents are moving too. Nicky's people have bought a place in Devon and Tom's have got a place in Wales."

"That's a coincidence," she said.

"I think Nicky's father feels just like Dad does. He's a banker. Perhaps they all know something." He wiped his mouth with the back of his hand. "I'll miss Brighton."

They reminisced about the good times they had all shared together in the house until she changed the mood by describing "Nodens", Athairton, and the mad party thrown for her by the villagers. Marcus grinned as she recounted O'Leary's rude "poem". "They sound great. I'm going to like living with the Tuatha De Danaan."

"The who?"

"Oh, Mum, you're so illiterate," he replied loftily. "They were the Celtic Gods."

"As a matter of fact there was a leader of the Celts called Lugh, so if your carpenter turns out to be their leader you'll probably find you're in the middle of a Celtic coven." He rolled on the floor. "Then Dad can fight his football hoolies with swords and spears."

"Come on you Celts, let's see to these oicks, shall we!" His impersonations of Chris were always cruelly accurate and despite her attempt to preserve some sort of respect for his father she eventually succumbed and joined him in his laughing antics. "And as for you, sir," Marcus danced around Mac like a gawky Nureyev, "If it comes to food shortages, don't think you won't be served up with an apple in your mouth."

The dog responded by throwing himself onto Marcus. During the ensuing rough and tumble, Isabelle detected the usual half-term tide mark, so delivered her regular lecture on adolescence and the need for thorough washing. Marcus immediately extricated himself from the dog and fled upstairs.

She listened to the sounds from the shower room. It could have been a sheep dip with Marcus' bleatings and Mac's sympathetic howls. A mournful "Cleanliness is Holiness" brought the unwelcome ablutions to an end and after exchanged banalities the house settled into its familiar stillness.

Clearing the lounge of boyish chaos, Isabelle thought over the events of the day. One incident forced her to remember Chris' warnings about the state of the country. It had happened while she and Marcus had been shopping together in Brighton. The boy had behaved peculiarly, speaking in a phoney accent and walking in a shambling, apelike way. When she had asked him why he was acting so strangely he had replied that he didn't like the looks he got when he spoke normally. Two of the sixth formers, he told her, had been beaten up when they had come into Brighton, for no other reason than their speech.

She thought about the strange uniformity of speech now prevalent among younger people. Was this the result of endless pop and drug-influenced fashion? Had the media's promotion of this culture successfully downgraded the language, creating the peer group dependence fearful of individuality? If this was so then Chris was right. An inarticulate people would have no other way of expressing their anger but through violence and the right political manipulation could lead them into civil war.

She contemplated her own difficulties in communication, seeing for the first time that her shyness was a guard against possible rejection. When she thought of Nodens and the welcome that she'd received from the villagers she felt relieved that Chris had made a decision to move. She remembered the glow that she had felt from their offered friendship, and how her fear of talking was removed, as she relaxed and enjoyed real laughter that always seemed such an effort when she attended the parties in London or Brighton. Her mind flitted from thought to thought until her drowsy meanderings were suddenly shattered by the memory of Chris and his final instructions about arranging a party.

Swirling torrents of confusion and panic forced her into the hall to look for pencil and paper. For the next two hours she sat drinking coffee and making guest lists until a low, drawn out moan from a mating cat reminded her that it was three o'clock and that she had a hectic day ahead of her with Marcus.

Lying in bed, listening to the flat discordant singing from the cats in the street below she thought of Old Sam.

What had he said about cats?

As she drifted off to sleep, she remembered that next month he'd be planting onions.

They sat carefully, balancing their supper plates on their knees and decorating the drawing room with their elegant, colourful, evening apparel.

As she watched them eating and listened to the gentle murmur of their refined voices, Isabelle was reminded of fading colonial society as depicted by American films. The house was stripped bare, allowing only the basic necessities for a party, everything else was packed efficiently into tea chests. It all added to the dramatic atmosphere of impending departure.

Chris hovered among the guests, happily expounding his views on declining Britain, and there were nodding heads of agreement between huge mouthfuls of food. Daphne flitted about helping to refill empty wine glasses and accepting gracefully the compliments for the cooking by some of the older, vaguer guests. Marcus, thrilled to be "out on bail" as he confided to Major Lawrence, stuffed with all the glee of a Billy Bunter and then retired early to bed.

Isabelle drifted between them all, feeling quite unreal. She was aware of herself being a perfectly dressed, empty shell.

The school motto that had hung on the walls of the convent,

daily burning its message into her brain, had said, "Her voice was ever soft and low, an excellent thing in women". Isabelle was a living credit to her convent upbringing as she floated, as it in a vacuum, amongst the guests, echoing their sentiments and gently agreeing with everything they had to say.

"Did you meet a sexy snowman or something?" Daphne was approaching her craftly. "What a funny thing to say," Isabelle replied unnerved that her vacant state of mind had been noticed.

"You've lost weight, gal, and you've been wafting round the house, with the expression of a sphinx, and I've always had my doubts about her." She had lost weight since her visit to Athairton, another four pounds. "I haven't been dieting," she replied. "It just happened."

"Chris suggested that I collect Marcus at the end of term and we all come down to Athairton together," Daphne went on, disappointed that there was no secret scandal to be shared. "What do you think?"

"Oh, that's wonderful," she replied, surprised that Chris had invited Daphne down to Athairton so quickly. Her forceful personality sometimes irritated him into a quick retreat into the study. "You'll be able to see it in its tumbledown state and then compare it when it's finished in the summer." She really was pleased about Daphne's intended visit. She knew that she would appreciate "Nodens", the gardens, and the little village. And Emma would be good company for Marcus.

The McAnallys wandered over to join them and commiserated over their departure. "Chris says he's sold the house." Professor McAnally stared at her inquisitively. "What are the people like, Isabelle?" A slow blush crept up from her neck to her cheeks. Guilt from the fact that Yehedi had nearly bought the house made her stutter. Thank God he'd changed his mind and bought a place in France, exonerating the Carringtons from any change in the Villa's way of life.

Instead, Chris had found a sober-minded accountant from the City who disagreed with all Chris' predictions about England and had jumped at the chance of owning the lovely old house. "I don't really know them," she replied hastily. "Chris knows him from his Gourmet club and seems to think he's very interesting."

"Let's hope he doesn't own a cat," Audrey McAnally moaned. "It's costing me a fortune in pepper dust to keep away the other foul monsters."

They then started to discuss the students' strike at the university, caused by the sacking of two of them. "Sometimes, I feel like emigrating," Professor McAnally said sadly. "Except Australia doesn't want any more British academics and Canberra is the only place I'd like to move to. I suppose I'm getting old and set in my ways."

They promised, as all the others guests had done, to visit them in Athairton. Isabelle found herself grinning inanely at the thought of a coachload of people from the Villas arriving for a party at "Nodens".

"Well, it seems to me you could always open a boarding house, Isabelle," said Daphne.

"Over my dead body!"

Her violent reaction to Daphne's joke shook them both. Flustered with embarrassment Isabelle excused herself and on the pretext of saying goodnight to Marcus retreated upstairs. Pausing on the landing, outside her son's bedroom, she was overcome with shame at snapping at her best friend in that way.

What had made her do it? Perhaps she was going off her head? She had, as Chris had observed, been behaving very strangely ever since they had first visited Nodens. She was becoming a changed person, even losing weight. She felt tearful and confused.

Marcus' room was a haven of schoolboy normality.

He sat in bed with a book, his mouth covered with the remains of Black Forest Gateau. "Escaping from the loonies, Mum?" he asked. "Marcus, do you think I'm odd?" she sighed, sitting on the end of the bed.

"Yes, of course you are," he replied. "So is Dad. He is really peculiar, you're just potty."

"How do you mean?" she asked, amazed at his confident appraisal of his parents. "Well, look at it this way." He placed his chin in his hands and sat looking like a wise Oberon.

"You're a smashing mum, I mean, when you and I are together, you are yourself but when you're with Dad or anyone else, you disappear."

"Disappear?"

"Yes, you don't exist. Dad on the other hand," he went on, "Exists loud and clear. He's a clever man but nuts. I like his cleverness but I don't like him."

She was shocked by his revelation.

"You don't like your own father?" she asked with horror.

"No, I don't. I used to be scared of him but now, I'm not scared any more, he's more or less just some man we know, who's clever but I feel nothing for." He looked at her carefully.

"Don't tell him though. I don't want to hurt his feelings. Lots of boys at school feel like I do about their parents, except I love you and a lot of them don't like their mothers either."

As she walked down the stairs to rejoin the party, she took in every detail of the hall. The lounge filled with the milling people was delicately and tastefully decorated but felt as empty and as hollow as she herself had felt earlier.

He had said that she didn't exist. Was that how other people saw her?

Catching the occasional, sparkling party eye, she acknowledged with a synthetic twinkle of her own. Daphne sidled over to her apprehensively. "Are you all right now? I'm sorry, I should have realised that you were feeling nostalgic. Trust me to put my foot in it."

"No, it was my fault," Isabelle said. "I don't know what came over me but I don't feel nostalgic. I just want to leave here, quickly."

After Chris had cleared away his antique wine glasses he retired to bed, leaving Isabelle to clear away the rest of the party debris. Shuffling around in her blue fluffy dressing gown she thought of the number of parties they had thrown where Chris had behaved in exactly the same way. First clearing away his own precious glasses and then leaving the rest to her.

A group of cats started to yowl outside in the street.

As she stacked the dishwasher she thought of the warm, happy informal party at Nodens. She had existed there. It would be different in Nodens she vowed to herself. That home would not be an empty shell of a house, with people visiting that she didn't give a damn about.

Remembering where Chris kept the air gun, she feverishly made her way to the cupboard in the study. Marcus had shown her how to load it.

She crept quietly into the bedroom where Chris lay, snoring loudly. Lifting the window quietly she looked down into the street.

They were poised in spiky, grotesque positions like a bunch of evil demons. Focusing the sights on the one in the middle she pulled the trigger.

As the crack sounded they scattered, leaving one still form in the middle of the road. A passing car's headlights picked up the lifeless body of the ginger tom.

CHAPTER SIX

March came in like a bad tempered lion, bringing an overwhelming vote of no confidence on the government from the strike-bound British. An air of excitement pervaded the coutryside as people discussed the impending election.

"I suppose they'll all vote for 'Our man for all people'," Chris commented sourly. They were watching one of the nightly party political broadcasts. A small, stocky man was emphasising his statements by jabbing his right forefinger at the listening crowd. "Listen to him Isabelle. He starts on a middle C and slowly works his way up the octave." The man's gesticulating quickened and the crowd responded wildly to his high-pitched final declaration. "Oh yes, he knows the value of the emotional note. It's the same technique that Hitler and Mussolini used. Any competent singer knows the art. To think we could fall into totalitarianism because of one oratorical busker." He applied, as usual, for his postal vote but Isabelle would have to return from Athairton for hers.

They made their colossal move in the second week of March. Chris immediately attacked all the problems like a feverish army captain as he organised the whole house for survival.

Nialls fitted the up-to-date lighting, exclaiming, "Well I never!" as he twiddled with the knobs for dimming the lights. O'Leary fixed up all the roofing and odd plumbing that needed attention and Lugh started to decorate. Isabelle watched him, he handled Chris with great tact but gentle firmness. Soon Chris was saying, "I think this funny green colour might be quite effective in the study." Or "Lugh suggested that this colour would be more restful in the bedroom and I'm inclined to agree with him." When the colour schemes were finally agreed, Isabelle took over the complementary furnishings.

Slowly, Nodens began to grow into a home. Old Karen came to

work for three days a week, the same days that Sam worked in the garden.

One day she explained her relationship with the old gardener. "I used to go steady with Sam when we were kids," she said. "But oh, I was naughty, I used to tease him so and make him jealous. Then he got himself married, so I did too, and the daft thing was, we both knew we'd done wrong, but there we are. Well, my husband, he were killed in the war, and his wife, she died last year. Mind you, she always knew really, well, the whole village knew. And now, well, I've lived on my own for so long I'm used to it. So I clean for him and everything and we court. We're too old to be married now, we'd rather remember, you see, but we court in the evening. In our hearts, we've always been married, ye see."

Old Sam cleaned out the little grotto and the conservatory that was attached to it. He had some wonderful ideas about climbing plants and drew up a list of them for her to buy. She asked Chris whether she could have the conservatory as her own private den and to her delight he agreed although he expressed his doubts about Old Sam's sanity after an incident that had happened one Saturday.

They had been woken up at five o'clock in the morning by strange noises coming from the garden. Chris had armed himself with a gun and a large torch and stormed bravely out into the darkness while Isabelle had remained inside the kitchen, shivering with fright. He had returned outraged. "He told me to shush," he announced to the trembling Isabelle.

"Who?" she asked, wondering why Mac had continued to sleep peacefully instead of rushing out to defend them. Chris then explained how he had found Old Sam, his pyjamas peeping out of the top of his old work clothes, muttering and digging in the kitchen garden. When Chris asked him what the hell he thought he was doing, he had been told to, "Shush, or you'll frighten them."

He was planting cabbages, he explained. "It was to be before the dawn on St. Patrick's Day, they'll head up well then." Chris had fled back to the kitchen, leaving him alone to continue with his muttering and planting and ever since then he had steered clear of the old gardener. Isabelle, however, listened with delight at everything that Sam told her.

"It's all to do with the stars and the moon, you see," he explained, as she watched him prune the rambling roses, "That's why there are definite times to plant. The animals and birds, now they understand, they do. Sometimes of course, Mother Nature now, she plays tricks, just to keep you on your toes, I think, but she always gives you a good warning."

Her led her down to the lawns. "See there," he pointed. "Even though this weather is bad, they were happy when they were planted. That was last year, before you knew you was coming here." Isabelle caught a glimpse of shy yellow, hiding behind the summer house. The first daffodil.

"Another couple of warm days and they'll be dancin'," he chuckled. Within a few days she and Old Sam shared the spectacular sight of the daffodil ballet as, after being warmed by the spring sunshine, they unfurled their yellow trumpets and jigged in the gentle southerly breeze. Tentative bluebells peeped from their green shoots as they waited for a warmer cue to make their entrance.

"Listen out for the cuckoo, won't you, there's one flies through those woods there," Sam told her.

"I will," she promised.

He beamed and started to clap his hands and stomp his feet.

"When you hear the cuckoo shout,

'Tis time to plant yer tetties out'," he chanted.

She joined him in his chant until he was sure she knew the rhyme, then he headed towards the apple trees and she made for the house. Chris' stereo music was playing at full volume. "The Karelia Suite comes to Nodens," she mused to herself.

A disembodied yellow cloth shook itself out of the lounge window where Karen was dusting. Baking smells wafted through the air, reminding her of the time, as she hurried back to the kitchen. A peaceful Mac lay sunning himself against the back door step.

Since moving a whole new world had opened up for the old dog — new scents, endless walks, a huge territory to defend, small animals to chase and the chickens.

David had brought some laying hens with some nesting boxes and Isabelle had to watch very carefully every time she let herself into the run in case the cunning old dog squeezed past her to satisfy his daily fantasy about biting their feathery bottoms.

The sound of Lugh's rich baritone voice came from the scullery. He stood there, singing happily and rinsing out his paint brushes. His sinewy arms tautened as he squeezed the brushes and muscles rippled through his woven shirt as his rib cage rose and fell with each fresh burst of song. He faltered, sensing her presence, and turned towards her. She found herself grinning stupidly at him.

"It's nearly spring," she commented inanely.

His eyes twinkled wickedly. "It makes you want to run like the mad March hare, doesn't it?"

"Yes," she giggled.

Flushing with embarrassment she returned to the kitchen just in time to take out the steak and kidney pies. He followed her, sniffing at the warm baking smells. "There's one each, for you, Karen and Sam," she reassured him.

How she would have liked to sit with them in the kitchen but Chris had been absolutely adamant about keeping a dividing line between friendliness and familiarity.

None of them had commented on her withdrawal to the dining room with Chris. In fact, Old Karen improvised with a menial subservient attitude to help her cope with the situation. She discreetly bobbed in and out of the room, helping Isabelle to serve and clear the table, while the glances of sympathetic understanding from the others made all thoughts of apology unnecessary.

Chris was in his element as lord of the manor. He'd put on weight since arriving at Nodens and acquired a shooting stick, which helped to promote his new image. "I'm going to plant a tree," he announced, as she sat down to lunch.

"There's a small yew growing down by the little bridge. I'm going to dig it up this afternoon. I would have asked Sam to do it but he's bound to have some daft reason or other to refuse. He really is quite insane, that man. I heard him singing to the apple trees this morning."

He arrived back at the house later that afternoon, breathless but triumphant. Then, clutching his tiny tree and armed with a spade and fork, he strode purposefully down to the far lawn, to plant it. Old Sam and Lugh were packing up, ready to leave. They stopped their conversation to watch Chris as he strode through the orchard on the way to the lawns.

Isabelle watched from the lounge window as Old Karen walked over to the others and joined them in a muffled conversation that was impossible to overhear from her position inside the lounge. They all turned suddenly and watched as Chris commenced digging.

An unexpected feeling of apprehension came over her, as she watched the three of them standing silently together.

The shadows were lengthening as the sinking, pale orange sun sent its last feeble rays across the horizon. Chris seemed to have finished his tree planting. The dying sunlight touched his fair hair as he walked slowly back to the house so that it resembled a moving halo.

Old Sam broke from the group to mount his bicycle and after ringing his bell to attract her attention he waved and shouted his goodbye. Lugh tucked Karen into his car and then crossed over to her. The cold, damp air penetrated her shoulders as she opened the window to him. "Sam was telling me that the conservatory's going to be your own private place, is that true?"

His dark blue eyes looked at her seriously.

"Yes," she replied, wondering whether that was what they had been discussing while Chris had planted his tree. "Would you like me to decorate it for you?" he asked gently. "In my own time," he added.

She flushed again with confusion. Part of her felt as if he was wanting some sort of commitment from her and yet, she also felt concerned that he should not think that she wanted to take advantage of his good nature. "Won't you be too tired?" she asked, blurting out the words.

His eyes glinted as he glanced towards the last sliver of light from the setting sun. He paused for a moment and then turned to smile at her. "I shall find it relaxing," he said.

He waved to her from the car as they drove away. She tried

to wave her hand but had to hold on to the window sill to stop the trembling that was overtaking her whole body. Her heart was pounding and even her bloodstream seemed to have changed its course.

She squeezed the bellows until the flames crept higher over the logs. Although the central heating was on it was still chilly and there was a dampness in the air that evening. She heard Chris stamping his feet in the scullery. "Isabelle," he shouted.

"Here," she replied. It was a very different Chris that came padding in to see her. With his dirty arran socks and mud-smeared face he reminded her of Marcus when he had been a toddler.

He held some daffodils in his hand as Marcus had once triumphantly held some young wallflowers calling them "Weeds".

"Will you put these in water?" he said. "Another week and there'll be bluebells as well." He wandered over to the window and looked out towards the lawns. A grey twilight blurred his view.

"I shall look at that tree when I'm an old man," he said proudly. "And I shall remember the day I planted it."

Daphne, Marcus and Emma arrived on the twenty-fifth of March. The quiet afternoon was shattered as they all shouted their approval and delight when they saw the house. After rushing all over the place Marcus and Emma made friends with Old Sam who, inspired by his young fresh-faced audience, reached even greater heights with his story-telling.

Daphne had bought a jasmine plant for Isabelle and after being shown the grotto insisted that it be planted there. "It can hang over the little statue," she said, her eyes looking lovingly at the gardener's paradise.

She spent the rest of the remaining daylight exploring the many small corners in the gardens, thrilled that she had a holiday stretching before her where she could make use of her green fingers. After dinner, Chris held court on the art of survival in the event of revolution then disappeared with Marcus to instruct him in strategy.

Later, when Isabelle kissed Marcus goodnight, he whispered, "You realise he's got an arsenal in his study, Mum. Bows and arrows and guns. He's drawn maps of Nodens and the places where we're going to set booby traps. He's even talking about buying geese. I think he's finally flipped."

The following day Chris drove up to London, promising to return after a couple of days. "Business," he said, "still has to go on, revolution or no revolution." It was a warm and sunny day so after lunch they decided to walk to Porlock Weir and back. As they sauntered through Athairton Daphne was full of enthusiastic appreciation.

"But it's ancient!" she cried. "It's as if time had stood still here. Even the people have a look about them, Isabelle, I can't quite put my finger on it, but it's. . ."

Isabelle felt very protective about Athairton. "It's just different from Brighton," she said defensively. Then, remembering vaguely how she had felt when she and Chris first drove through the village, she added, "I think I thought it was strange when I first saw it but now it just seems restful."

Daphne lapsed into a silent watchfulness.

As they crossed the moors, early lambs stumbled and leant against their woolly mothers. The occasional rabbit scampered into the brush, hiding from the sparrow hawk that hovered high above them. Wild ponies scattered as Mac chased them, yapping happily. By the time they reached Porlock Weir their faces were pink with exertion and Mac's tongue was drooping near the ground.

"A pause," Daphne gasped, as Marcus and Emma headed towards the track for Culbone. She spread her bottom on to an accommodating wall.

"It's all very well for you, Marcus Carrington. You're used to great hikes and cross country runs," she heaved, filling her lungs with air, "but some of us," she panted, "the most some of us walk, is a quick dash to the shops and back. Oh, God," she sighed.

Isabelle was thrilled to discover that she was far fitter then Daphne. Used to regular walks into the village with Mac, not only had she lost more weight but her legs had become quite sturdy. Daphne's face was beginning to turn a deep scarlet. Isabelle felt a bit mean about having put her through such an assault course on her first day.

"Are you feeling all right?" she asked guiltily.

"Don't worry," Daphne muttered. "It's only a quick flush."

The track to Culbone wound its way steeply through a thick forest. Looking down to their right, through tall pines, they caught sight of the sea below, shimmering in the afternoon sunshine. Fallen leaves and moss made the pathway fairly slippery, forcing them to clutch wildly at tree trunks as they passed in order to regain their balance.

Marcus and Emma found an old stone lookout and proceeded to climb all over it while Daphne and Isabelle slipped on at a steady pace. "This is a strange area, Isabelle," said Daphne as they slipped on. "I'm not fey but I've had some definitely strange feelings since I've been here."

"In what way?" Isabelle said. "Well," she grabbed a tree trunk to steady herself and gazed down towards the sea. "I had a strange dream last night, so did Emma. In fact we both woke up at the same time, about two o'clock. She came into my room."

Isabelle's pulse quickened.

"What did you dream?" she asked, biting her lip.

"Well, I dreamt someone was pulling me somewhere, so did Emma, and I fought back, then I woke up."

Isabelle was silent as the thoughts winged through her mind. "Have you had any more of those funny experiences that you told me about?" Daphne went on. Isabelle sighed with relief at the thought of sharing the dream.

As they continued walking she told her about the strange child and how she felt drawn towards her.

"Ah."

Daphne assumed the knowing air of the expert coffee table occultist. "It's haunted," she declared. "Well it was bound to be. It's so old that house. I should think they're running all over the place," she gurgled gleefully. "We ought to have a seance and see what we can get."

"Oh, I don't think Chris would like that," Isabelle replied quickly. "In fact I don't think I would. Perhaps they'll go away after we've lived there for a time. I must say, I don't mind the dreams so much now, in fact I quite look forward to them. I want to see her face."

"That could be dangerous," Daphne warned her.

Half an hour later they came upon Culbone. It was a small hamlet, consisting of three tiny thatched cottages and a miniature church. The track they were walking on led down to an old bridge under which two small streams met then rushed noisily down to the sea.

Their pathway forked as it came to the bridge. One way led along to the left of the stream, following its course upwards through thick forests, and the other continued across the bridge. At the other side of the bridge, the track divided again. One pathway wound backwards and up a steep gorge towards Athairton, the other led to the old cottages and the church.

Marcus and Emma caught up with them as they reached the entrance to the church. Mac tottered towards a gravestone and flopped down on to it. Inside the church there was only enough room to seat about sixteen people.

Daphne collapsed on to a pew, sighing with relief, while Marcus and Emma examined the old Norman font and Isabelle ran her fingers over carved the oak chancel screen. "My God," Daphne moaned, "you'd have to be fit to attend this church."

Emma was enchanted. "It's beautiful, Mum, it's like a church for dolls."

Coming out of the church again, Daphne spotted a sign with TEAS written on it and a wooden arrow pointed to one of the cottages. Her eyes lit up and she approached the cottage like a lost desert wanderer.

An old woman, who looked about ninety, peered at them, then smiling her approval ushered them to a bench and wooden table outside and agreed to "a pot of tea for four and a saucer for the dog". Isabelle sat quietly puffing a cigarette, waiting for the tea to arrive, when she was suddenly grabbed by Daphne.

"My God! Do you realise," she whispered, "the rivers meet where the roads cross. That's magic. It's a sign of magic ground."

The trio of females enthused and romanced about Culbone's possible magic history while Marcus looked on scornfully. The old lady returned with the tea and some freshly made queen cakes, her wrinkled face wreathed in smiles. "She's probably used to potty tourists imagining they could see things popping out of the stream," Marcus commented cynically.

They took the right hand fork which led them back, uphill through the forest and on to the moor, where a road twisted down into Athairton. They were tired now and the track was much rougher. Marcus and Emma led the way, occasionally yanking their respective mothers over tricky mounds and slippery patches of mud.

Culbone slowly disappeared back into the tree-fringed gorge. Dappled moments of sunshine became steady warmth as they climbed higher and into the sunlight.

"Mum, look!" Marcus pointed to a strange, igloo-shaped house, built into the hill.

Pulling back some branches, they saw herds of cows grazing on the slope below the house. A large round chimney stuck out of the top of the strange dome-like building, like the stalk of a mushroom. Huge windows, reflecting the sunshine, gave the dome-like shape the appearance of having eyes.

In the middle of the lawn in front of the house grew a large oak. To the left of the tree was an ornamental lake surrounded by statues. Skirting the house was a large, circular patio with stone objects standing on it that from the distance appeared to be sun dials.

About half a mile away, in the other direction, stood a cluster of barns and outhouses.

"What an extraordinary building!" Isabelle remarked. "It must be some sort of modern design." They were out of the trees now and looking back down towards the odd-shaped place.

There was the tinkling sound of a bell and the cows began to drift together and make their way slowly towards the barns. Marcus found the sign, tucked into the hedge. WHITEHOUSE FARM.

They stood watching the slowly moving herd.

She appeared suddenly on the patio. A tall woman in a flowing cream robe. Her hair was a vivid red and shone in the sunshine. It was hard to determine her age but from her body's agile movements she appeared to be about thirty. Swiftly she ran towards the herd, her hair flowing like a red streamer behind her.

Her wild shouts mingled with the bellowing of the cattle.

Marcus was entranced.

Emma, Isabelle and Daphne were fascinated by the abandoned behaviour of the strange woman. She disappeared into the shadows of the barns, the last straggling cows hurrying to catch up with her.

"Well, that's made me feel quite ancient," Daphne said sourly, pulling herself up the track. "What an extraordinary woman. I wonder who she is?".

"I'll ask Sam." Isabelle was puzzled. Part of her had felt that she knew the woman from somewhere, but she couldn't understand how, or from where she had known her.

It was dusk when they reached Athairton. Daphne was practically on her knees as they stagged down the road. Arthur O'Leary waved to them from his work shed.

"Evening Mrs. Carrington. My but ye look worn out."

Isabelle leaned against the wall and agreed with him, explaining between gasps how they had walked the round route to Culbone and back. "Hold on a minute and I'll run you home in the van." He disappeared inside the house.

"Oh, thank God," Daphne sighed as she leant against the wall. Marcus and Emma left the panting mothers and wandered into the shed to satisfy their curiosity.

Gwynneth popped her head out of the rose-covered porchway. "Mrs. Carrington, you look worn out. Look, I've got a large stewpot going, so would you like to rest yourselves and then have some rabbit stew. Arthur will run you to your house later."

Pungent cooking aromas wafted out of the door towards them. Daphne groaned. "I'm starving," she whispered. "Do you think she really means it or is she just being polite?".

"Are you sure?" asked Isabelle. "There's four of us you know".

"And Mac," Gwynneth smiled at the old Cairn who was panting by the gate. "Yes of course I'm sure. There's a huge pot going, come on in".

Inside the small thatched cottage was a cosy parlour room with low oak beams. Gwynneth led them to two comfortable armchairs and then brought them some elderflower wine. "That'll give you a lift," she said, winking conspiratorially.

Isabelle closed her eyes and relaxed into the soft armchair.

Through the window she could hear Marcus and Emma asking Arthur all sorts of questions. She listened to the sound of his deep drawling voice and the ringing sound of iron on steel as he answered them and beat out horseshoes at the same time.

The room smelt of heather. Bunches of dried flowers fanned from triangular pots, arranged side by side on the stone window sill. Corn dollies hung from the beams and little carved wooden figures stood in groups on the oak mantelpiece. She felt too comfortable to get up and examine them but one looked very like the wooden figurine standing in the grotto at Nodens.

They had both dozed for a while when Gwynneth came bustling back into the room. "It's all ready," she said. "I just had a few more tetties to do." Around the table, lit by an old oil light, they all joined in their praises for Gwynneth's rabbit stew.

Damson wine was produced and soon the room was filled with the same warmth that she had experienced with the party at Nodens. Arthur told more rhymes and Marcus laughed so much that at one time he was nearly in danger of rolling off his chair. Eagerly he swapped his jokes from school, and as he and Arthur egged each other on the shouting became more raucous than ever. Even Daphne was quite pickled with the effects of the wine and the tiredness from her long walk.

There was a lull while Gwynneth served a wonderful treacle pudding and Isabelle asked them about the strange woman with the red hair. Arthur's amused expression changed to one of respect. "That's Bridget," he said quietly.

"Oh yes, you'll be meeting her," Gwynneth echoed his tone. "She's the wise one."

Then changing the subject she asked, "Is there anyone who could eat a second helping?" There was a shout of gluttonous approval from Marcus who immediately proceeded to sing a ridiculous pudding song. The rest of the evening passed happily with more silly songs.

Bloated and contented, they were driven back to Nodens, with Mac hanging over Isabelle's shoulder, snoring fitfully. Even the sounds of the water system, calming down after their joint assault before retiring to bed, gave a belch of gurgling approval for their merry evening.

There was a tap on Isabelle's door and Daphne came in, her face all smothered in night cream. "You realise she's a witch, don't you? I mean, I didn't dare ask because frankly, I was a bit pissed and I thought I might giggle and they were both so respectful, but love, 'wise woman', that's another name for witch, isn't it?" They sat on the bed, speculating wildly on Bridget's possible powers, until giggling hysterically they both retired to their beds.

March went out like an undecided lamb. The cuckoo that Old Sam promised would come arrived shouting loud and clear. "I suppose the whole of Athairton is out planting potatoes," Chris commented drily.

The blackthorn flowered, which worried Old Sam. "Ee sometimes fools ye. After ee flowers, sometimes the frost comes back," he muttered.

Marcus became really involved with the villagers and often disappeared early in the morning down to O'Leary's where he could help him shoe horses or wandered around with Sam, helping him to mix soot for the garden. "Sam's so clever, Dad," he informed Chris. "His methods of gardening are far better and safer than the use of dangerous chemicals. I'm taking notes on everything he uses, for the conservation society at school."

"You don't realise what our generation is going to have to cope with when your generation dies out. Pollution, mineral shortages and general danger to the environment through sheer stupidity." Chris listened to Marcus carefully and gained a new respect for what he had considered to be an insane old man.

June gave birth to a nine pound baby boy on the fifth of April.

Isabelle found out from Karen that Maeve, the barmaid, was the "best knitter" locally and with Daphne went to visit her in the small cottage where she lived with her parents. They were treated to a display of baby clothes that could have rivalled Harrods, so after buying a collection of blue and white baby clothes they set off to visit June at the Taunton maternity home and spent the whole afternoon crowing over the newest Carrington.

After Sam's expected few days of frost, the air grew warmer and the orchard burst into flower. He was especially pleased when the mulberry tree blossomed. "Now this is the wise old tree," he said approvingly. "Ee isn't silly like some of those trees that puts out their leaves early and gets nipped. Ee waits 'til the frost's over."

The mornings were her favourite time of day. Woken by the gentle squawks from the chickens she would leave the sleeping Chris and pad softly downstairs with Mac. On her own in the kitchen, she would quietly lay out the breakfast table and then, taking her coffee and cigarettes, walk through to the walled garden to sit on the wooden bench and commune with the new day.

This morning, watching the bright flashes of the goldfish as they sought the warm dappled patches of sunlight, she marvelled at the fact that within such a short space of time she should feel such a powerful sense of belonging.

With the people in Athairton she felt so at ease, as if in some way she had found a large family which she was part of, and yet never known. Her fear of talking had gone. She surprised herself a week earlier when she found herself chattering in Nialls' store, sharing a thought which, before then, she would never have voiced. Sometimes she would even forget to have a cigarette, being so engrossed with the daily activities.

A yellow wagtail ran inside the small clearing, looking cautiously at her before striding quickly on his thin legs to seize an early morning worm.

A slight movement from the corner of her eye caused her to turn.

The little girl ran through the garden and into the grotto.

She gasped with shock.

With shaking hands, she tried to place the coffee down on the bench as quietly as she could.

Had she imagined it?

Her heart pounded as she crossed towards the entrance of the grotto and peered inside.

She was there, her little blonde head bowed over the wooden figurine.

Isabelle held her breath, she felt that she could almost reach out and touch her.

"Who are you?" she asked breathlessly.

The child ignored her and without turning round, got up and walked into the conservatory.

Isabelle followed, feeling that she was taking part in some extraordinary dream.

There was no one in there.

She paused to look around and slowly became aware of the walls. There was her mind, exposed on brick, in picture form. Symbols that summoned up memories from deep within her subconscious.

Her dreams, formed in paint by Lugh.

She reeled with dizziness.

Holding her head and breathing deeply, she began to examine the painting. The tunnel that she passed through every night, leading to the field. Moving closer, she saw an oak tree, where a woman stood bound by a loose cord of silk around her neck. She traced the cord through the tree towards a herd of cows. There, sitting in the middle of the herd, was a youth with antlers. He was smiling, the cord passing through a gold ring through his tongue. Looking closer at the smiling youth she could see that it was Lugh.

Who was the woman bound by the silk cord? She felt that she knew her very well but couldn't remember her name or from where it was that she knew her.

CHAPTER SEVEN

Old Sam remained adamant. He refused to allow Daphne to plant the parsley. It was Isabelle, he insisted, who should plant it and even then, it should only be planted on Good Friday.

He had planted hazel sticks all over the garden, against any evil he informed them, and he "weren't have it undone by no parsley."

Apart from Chris, who was appalled at the "arrogant old bugger", everyone was quite willing to humour the old man and Isabelle planted the parsley seeds late in the afternoon on Friday the thirteenth, with a drop of holy water from the church, as Old Sam had instructed her.

They had all attended the early morning mass, Chris insisting that as the new owners of Nodens "we should be seen to support the church". The Reverend Morrigan was overjoyed to see them. It was understandable as there were only three other people in the congregation.

"I suppose everyone comes to the Sunday service," Chris said, in an attempt to put the vicar at ease. "Oh, no," the vicar replied benignly, "they never come. These people are holiday makers," he said, indicating the three departing visitors who were slowly making their way to their respective cars.

"Please don't misunderstand me," he added quickly. "This village is the warmest-hearted parish that I've ever known. It's just that they'd rather go down to the pub," he grinned. Isabelle agreed with him that it was a very kind village but when Marcus and Emma had been invited to an Easter party to be held in the village hall she had naturally assumed that it had been arranged by the church.

"Oh gracious no!" said the vicar. "I shall be going of course, but everything like that is always organised by Bridget."

Daphne interrupted.

"Isn't that the woman from Whitehouse Farm?"

"Yes," the vicar smiled.

"Is she a witch?"

The Reverend Morrigan assumed the bland expression of a well-trained marriage guidance counsellor. "She's a very wise woman, who inspires great community spirit," he said calmly. "Now if you'll excuse me, there's a chess tournament I've got to watch."

"Chess?" Marcus' ears pricked up. Next to riding, chess was his most favourite hobby. The vicar's face came to life.

"Are you interested in chess?" he asked. "Oh yes, would you mind if I came with you? If that's all right with you, Dad?"

Chris was only too pleased. Chess was a game of which he thoroughly approved and he was very proud of his son's exceptional talent for it.

On the way home, Daphne analysed Athairton's goings on as if she were a *News of the World* reporter.

"If this woman Bridget is a witch," Chris commented, "we'll get her to do this water divining lark. I'd quite like our own well, if possible." He then firmly called a halt to any further discussion about Bridget.

Marcus didn't arrive back until teatime. He wandered into the kitchen just as Isabelle was taking a batch of hot cross buns out of the oven. Chris asked him how he'd fared in the tournament.

"Well, it wasn't like a usual tournament. There was no feeling of competition, more a kind of sharing." He concentrated on buttering his bun. "First we played people the same level as ourselves, then we played the beginners to help them learn." He munched thoughtfully. "We talked about chess being like the world. That it was like the universe inside ourselves. She told us how the opponent was like a part of our mind. She said we had to understand. . ."

"Who?"

"Oh, Bridget, she's all right."

Marcus watched with humour as his news had the expected impact. Like a Chancellor answering questions before Budget day, he strolled round the kitchen, chewing his bun carefully before giving any information.

Much to everyone's disappointment, all they could glean from the interrogation, was that Bridget was O.K. "Sort of any age, touched them on the head a lot and her skin smelt lovely when you were near."

Chris remembered a quote from the Koran and disappeared off to the study.

The twilight was reaching further into the evenings. After planting the parsley, Isabelle and Daphne strolled round the gardens continuing their gossip. While Daphne speculated on the history of Athairton, Isabelle felt momentary sadness. In another week they would all be leaving. Chris would be departing for Bahrain on the eighteenth and Daphne, Marcus and Emma would be setting off on the twenty-fourth. It had been such a pleasant time. Daphne being at Nodens had certainly helped her to survive Chris' changing moods. Or was it, as Daphne had told her, that she herself was changing.

They had been crossing the lawn when a squadron of migrant birds wheeled across the sky. She and Daphne had stood watching them as they grouped and regrouped into moving patterns. "It's beautiful here, Isabelle," she had said. "And you know, I think it's doing an awful lot for you, despite all the peculiar things that seem to happen."

Isabelle pulled a money spider from the conifer's spiky needles and watched it dangle on the end of the finely spun thread. "I mean for instance," Daphne continued, "you're much more talkative than you used to be. You used to be the one person that I could rely on to listen to me rant on for ever," she laughed. "But now, do you know, you actually interrupt." Isabelle smiled at the thought of anyone actually interrupting Daphne.

She was right however, about how she had changed. Especially in her attitude towards Chris.

When they had been living in Clifton Villas and he had gone into one of his silent angry moods, she would have sunk into despondency, feeling automatic guilt for being the cause of his mood. Here in Nodens she found herself ignoring his depressions as she carried on with her activities and being unconcerned whether or not he sorted himself out.

She knew that Lugh had a lot to do with her newly found independence, as Daphne had been quick to point out.

"I think it's wonderful, love, to have a marvellously handsome young man painting your dreams. My sexologist used to explain mine and that's not half as romantic."

She had traced the shape of the symbols with her fingertips. "These, if I'm not mistaken, are Celtic. I've seen them in pictures of Iona or somewhere. I wonder what they mean?"

After supper, Isabelle and Daphne sat in front of the fire, cutting up pieces of yellow duster for Emma to appear as a daffodil at the Easter party. Marcus had borrowed an old blue jellabah from Chris and strung some old coca cola tins round his waist. He was going as an Easter daytripper. Daphne had put on weight during the holiday and moaned, as she stitched the dusters, that she would have to return to Weight Watchers as soon as she got back home to Brighton.

Isabelle's problem was the reverse. She had continued to lose weight and her clothes were getting baggy. When she returned to Brighton to vote she would buy some new clothes and visit the hairdressers.

The week flew past and Chris departed for Bahrain.

Isabelle drove him to Taunton station.

Watching his train pull away from the platform she felt a moment's regret which was replaced by a surge of relief as the train grew smaller in the distance. She felt sad that she was unable to feel anything more than a minor emotion about Chris' departure but then emotions have to be fed and nourished like plants and hers had been shut away, over the years, held captive in a very dark cupboard.

She bought a selection of things for Marcus' tuckbox and some batteries for his radio. There was a spring in her step as she wandered around the different counters of the large department store.

Having found a colourful wooden rattle she decided to call in and see June on the way back.

June was sitting on the sofa like a chubby Buddha.

On the soft blanket on the floor the baby lay gurgling and kicking his legs jerkily while the girls, who were thrilled to have a baby brother, ministered to him. June oversaw the joint maternalism and issued her instructions regally from her lofty position.

The rattle was gratefully received. Then promises were made for the Carringtons to come to Nodens for the following Sunday's lunch, David threatening to bring the cockerel that he'd promised for Chris.

Dawn came but she didn't hear the chickens.

Being on her own again she had slept deeply and heavily, as if catching up with an exhaustion of which she had been unaware.

She was woken by someone stroking her hair.

Marcus seemed to be holding the sun. Her eyes began to focus. He was clutching a huge posy of primroses. On the bedside table he had placed a tray of tea and toast.

"Happy primrose day, Mum."

"Primrose day?"

There was a squawk from Daphne's room as she was woken in the same way by Emma.

"Arthur told us that it's the custom here to give mothers primroses on the nineteenth. He showed us how to tie them." They were told to flop and enjoy being spoilt while Emma and Marcus looked after the house and cooked the meals.

They spent a contented languid day, appreciating the wisdom of Athairton's customs.

Early bees explored the sweetly smelling wallflowers. A martin swooped through the walled garden. They sat, drinking coffee and listening to the crashes coming from the kitchen as Emma and Marcus prepared lunch.

"You're not in love with Chris, are you?"

Daphne was squinting into the sun.

"Why do you say that?"

"I don't know. I suppose I've always assumed that you were the one couple whose marriage really worked ... but then, I hadn't stayed with you for four weeks before. Your marriage is as empty as mine was with Tony, isn't it?"

"I don't know." Isabelle shut her eyes and wondered how to change the subject.

"Why don't you have an affair with Lugh?"

It occured to Isabelle that Daphne had used the same intonation as if she were advising her to change her washing powder.

"I should think he's bloody marvellous in the feathers."

Isabelle felt herself blushing.

The image of Sister Mary Helen's red face appeared, threatening them with the dreaded mortal sins as they prayed on their knees in the school hall. The horror of the memory made her shudder.

Daphne misinterpreted her reaction.

"Oh, I thought you fancied him," she chirped.

"I'm sorry?"

Isabelle pulled her concentration back to Daphne's thread of conversation.

"No, I don't think I could fool around with Lugh," she said, blushing again. "It wouldn't be fair," she added lamely.

"Suit yourself," Daphne replied nonchalantly. "Mind you, if it's a hot summer and I come visiting, you won't mind if I bring a rope ladder, will you?" She kicked her feet in the air which caused Mac to growl with irritation.

Isabelle found the idea amusing and joined in with the laughter, but for the first time in their relationship an uneasy jealousy slimed across her stomach.

Her mind darted back to the horrendous memory of convent days that had disturbed her earlier. It had been squashed for years, back into the recesses of her mind and covered by a thick emotional web which protected her from nightmares. Why had it been pulled out? What unseen war was provoking her mind to throw up these revelations?

They had a wonderful lunch which deserved a visit to the cinema to aid their digestion.

They all traipsed off to an afternoon of fantasy with an indulgence of ice-creams and sweets.

That night she felt such urgency.

Desperately, she tried to push past the herd of cows to the waiting child.

She tried shouting to her but could only send a slight wind that reached out to ruffle the fair hair.

The unseen arms, whose strength had brought her to the field, let her go and she felt herself floating as aimlessly as a dandelion seed, drifting on the back of the wind.

Panic.

She felt as if she was going to be swept into a vast sea of blackness, forever.

Back she fell into the churning mud. Where were her lungs? She couldn't breathe.

Isabelle woke up sweating with fright.

Mac whined and rushed over to console her. She clung to the little dog with relief, grateful for even his halitosis that brought her back to the world of the living.

The chickens tilted their heads coyly and watched the extrovert young cockerel stalk around his new territory. Marcus roared with laughter. "It's like Dad, seeing if we've moved anything while he's been away."

David and June appreciated the likeness and promptly christened the cockerel Christopher Columbus. There had been three rather frosty nights in a row. Sam, of course, had anticipated them and covered his precious seedlings way before the event, which really impressed David and June.

Over lunch, Marcus earnestly discussed with David Old Sam's ideas about the crops being influenced by the planets and explained his project on the subject. They talked well into the afternoon on how the idea could revolutionise farming methods. Isabelle watched them striding about the garden, their heads lowered in deep discussion.

Marcus had enjoyed his holiday. Never before had she seen him so happy. His holidays in Brighton had never really stimulated him. Here, he had been in the company of rural craftsmen, who had talked to him as a young man and not a schoolboy.

Lugh had arrived at the house, two days after Marcus' chess tournament, carrying a beautifully carved chess table which he had presented to him. Later that evening she had watched him lovingly arrange his chess on the polished table top. The sight made tears come to her eyes.

Lugh had behaved like a father to him, patiently teaching him the skills of carpentry and archery. He had even made him a sling, which Marcus could now use with deadly accuracy. She wished that Chris could have had the same patience with Marcus that Lugh had shown, then he would have had an adoring son instead of an indifferent one.

After noisy farewells and promises from David that Marcus could have a summer holiday job with him on the farm the Carringtons departed in a cloud of dust.

She and Marcus wandered down to the summer house for a few precious moments on their own. She watched him lovingly as he confided in her his hopes for the future. He was half boy, half man. His downy face would soon grow stubble and then he would be another man, let loose on the world, to challenge life.

He wanted to be a farmer, but how would Chris react to his decision? His father had high hopes that he would follow his footsteps and study law. "You must live your own life," Isabelle advised, marvelling at the wisdom that she could offer, yet not understand herself.

Listening to Marcus as he extolled Lugh's virtues over supper Daphne remarked that it was interesting that he had never married. She had been following him around all week until Isabelle had become quite irritated. "She's behaving like one of the chickens," she had thought peevishly to herself.

"He's betrothed," Marcus explained to them.

"Betrothed?" Daphne blurted out.

"Those were the words he used," Marcus went on, in a matter of fact tone. "'I've been betrothed for years'. That's what he said."

The effect on the women was shattering.

Marcus pondered about it later as he packed his case for school and came to the conclusion that woman really were a funny lot.

The house was empty.

After two hours of tears and cigarettes she pulled herself together and drew up a schedule of things to do. After all, she reasoned with herself, hadn't Robinson Crusoe survived by the use of self-discipline.

Calm again, after the arduous task of listing all the food to be replenished, she threw on her mackintosh and started walking towards Athairton with Mac trotting happily at her side. A small crocodile of children passed her as she walked across the road to

Nialls' stores. Clutched in their small fists were bunches of primroses, daisies and other wild flowers. They chatted gaily together, their small faces full of merriment as they made their way to the old village school.

Lugh emerged from his cottage carrying a light wooden frame of uprights that supported graduated hoops. The structure was about four feet high and resembled a bell. He smiled as she waved to him, acknowledging her with a nod, then still clutching his wooden bell he disappeared into the school.

Maeve was standing by the dairy counter, deeply engrossed in conversation with two other women whom Isabelle had never seen before. Mr. Nialls was balanced precariously up a ladder. She joined the group with a "Good morning."

"Ah, Mrs. Carrington."

Maeve's round face was pink with animation. "Did you see them with their flowers?" she asked. "You'll be joining us I hope. There'll be no sleep on Monday night, it'll be all go."

"What's happening?"

She felt herself begin to get caught up in the excitement.

"May Day," Maeve replied. "I've got to get my lot of flowers this afternoon. We're decorating the bell for the Lady, for the procession."

"Is there anything I can bring?" Isabelle volunteered. "We haven't met yet." A bright-eyed little woman resembling a small rabbit pushed herself forward. "I'm Mrs. Morrigan, the vicar's wife. Do you by any chance have any spare white daisies in your garden?"

"I've masses," Isabelle replied, relieved that she wasn't going to be asked to make things with paper. She hated twisting bits of coloured tissue into flowers for women's organisations. "We need them for the queen's crown," Mrs. Morrigan explained.

"Where shall I bring them?" Isabelle asked, intrigued by the puckering lines that ran down Mrs. Morrigan's chin.

"Bring them Monday evening," Maeve chimed in. "We'll all be working at the school, getting the bell ready."

"I'd love to help," she smiled.

"Well if you've any red flowers could you bring those too?"

Isabelle agreed. She wandered out of Nialls' stores, laden with groceries and immediately regretted not bringing the car. "Oh you are stupid," she muttered to herself.

Mac had found the black labrador from the Tuatha Arms and was careering around the oak tree. She called him and he immediately shot off in the other direction.

She stood in the road, dithering about whether to ask Mr. Nialls to deliver the groceries, when a soft voice said, "Let me carry them."

"Where's your car?" Lugh asked her, glancing towards the parking space by the pub. "Like a fool, I left it behind. I can't think where my brains have gone today."

"Come back and have a coffee at my place and then I'll run you home." She hesitated, uncertain of the village protocol and, also, her own reaction.

Her body began to perspire with apprehension.

He made the decision for her, whistling for Mac, who came to him immediately and clung lovingly to his leg. He took her firmly by the arm and led her to his cottage. As the road wound its way out of the small village, it circled inwards towards a crossroad. The cottages sloped in ascendancy, perching on banks of hewn-out rock.

Rough steps twisted up from the road to join a steep pathway which, after levelling out by Lugh's gateway, descended again to become the rough tracks that skirted along the side of the country lane.

Stone walls enclosed the small garden that composed of a neat vegetable patch, herb garden and bowers of rambling roses. In the dark corners by the wall grew lupins, hollyhocks and wild bells. A horseshoe was nailed to a beam inside the small thatched porch. Stones, with natural holes through them, hung from wires attached to the thick outside walls.

Birds sauntered in the garden, confident of their safety. Mac chased them away and then after peeing over the lupins scampered into the living room to join them.

The room was small. Gleaming copper hung on the walls and from the open fire came the pleasant smell of burning peat. Draped over the backs of the two comfortable easy chairs were smooth deerskins. Over the mantel and challenging the whole room hung a pair of antlers.

Isabelle rubbed her cheek against the deerskin as she sat listening to the sounds of Lugh making coffee in his kitchen. "Did you hunt these deer?" she called.

"Yes," he shouted, "and there'll be another soon after Beltine, if I'm lucky." He brought in the coffee and pulled up the chair opposite her.

"Beltine?" she asked. "What's that?"

"You'd call it May Day, I suppose."

She told him how she'd been asked to help with the flowers on the Monday night. "That's only the beginning," he told her. "We've got to catch a deer, before the maypole goes up, so that everyone can have a barbecue. He went on to explain that Beltine was a great village festivity with parades, Morris dancing, children's plays and it ended with a dance in the village hall.

"You'll enjoy it," he added.

She was aware, that if she went to the dance, she would be a woman on her own, without a partner. As she sat drinking her coffee her inhibitions came crowding back, making all thoughts of attending the dance an awful nightmare. He watched her changing expressions thoughtfully, as if probing her mind. "Would you like to come as my partner?"

"Oh," she was startled. "But what about your fiancee, won't she mind me tagging along?"

"My what?"

Her face flushed with embarrassment. "Oh, I thought you were ... that is, Marcus told me, that you were ... that is ... um, 'betrothed'."

The very word squeezed itself between her lips. She felt as if she had been caught spying on him. He started to laugh.

"Ah." Then seeing her confusion, he paused.

"Yes, I'm betrothed, but she'd be more than happy if I took you to the dance."

He started to laugh again. How could he laugh about being engaged? "Will she be there?"

He looked at her. A wistful look appeared in his eyes. "In spirit," he said softly.

Changing the subject abruptly, he asked her whether she

would like to see his studio.

The stairway leading upstairs was narrow and curved sharply. A small passage led towards two doors. The one on the right opened into a tiny bathroom, the other revealed a large studio. Light streamed into the room through a large slanting skylight, the sides of which were fringed with the outside thatching.

Pieces of sculpture were arranged on the shelves. Paintings of scenes from the countryside, flowers and studies of birds lay scattered along the walls. Collages of vivid symbols, similar to the ones painted on her conservatory wall, hung on a wall in contrast with the soft-toned landscapes hanging on the opposite side.

Deerskins covered his bed which was tucked under the eaves. On the wall above it hung an ancient spear. Isabelle touched the sculptured head of an infant. "Is this your own work?"

"Yes, do you like it?"

"It's beautiful."

She wandered towards a small recess in which stood a bronze cauldron surrounded by minute wooden figures. "Oh," she exclaimed, running her hands over the cauldron, "this is exquisite."

She knelt on the floor and gently lifted it towards her. The metal felt almost sensual in her hands. Cupping it gently she looked inside. Something almost like an electric shock passed through her.

"Wait," he said.

She watched him as he lit a candle and placed it beside her. Then he drew a blind across the skylight. "You'll appreciate it better now," he said, kneeling beside her. "Tell me what do you see?"

The candlelight flickered across the bronze, creating a warm glowing world of imaginary pictures. She turned it. The child inside her surged forward to claim the moment of wonder, as slowly pictures began to form.

Without warning, she fell into the tunnel and sped towards the pinprick of light that nightly opened so that she could pass into the field, where the child sat waiting for her.

The arms that usually pulled her through tightened and began pulling her away from the light. The male smell surged into her senses and a soft gentle voice spoke as she was pulled further back. "You're not ready to go there yet, trust me."

He was holding her tightly and smoothing her brow. When he saw that she was all right he gently released her.

"We'll solve that dream of yours," he said, as he drew the blind, "but not now."

"Then it's not the house?" she asked, struggling to her feet. "It's gone on so long, Lugh, ever since I first told you about it. It comes every night." It was strange. He had so much natural authority. It was almost as if he was older than her.

He reached for her hand as she followed him down the stairs. "Careful," he warned her, "the steps are narrow."

His hand sent the most wonderful warmth through her arm.

He had asked her to trust him and she did. A whole area of her mind, that had ached with loneliness for so many years, felt healed.

When they reached Nodens he turned to her and cupping her face in his hands gazed into her eyes. "You won't have any more dreams until Monday, so just relax and enjoy life."

He paused. "And after your flower group has finished, we'll solve that dream so that you can really enjoy Beltine."

CHAPTER EIGHT

Endless party political broadcasts promoted people whom Isabelle found quite unbelievable.

On the news, cameras showed preparations around the world for May Day. World leaders presented their macabre pageant. Processions of National plays showed military acrobatics with spectacular displays of weaponry. Crowds of unemployed waved brightly painted banners and marched to the rhythm of their anger. Affluent and degenerate clowns celebrated their obesity and obscenity, while standing in the wings was dark-eyed consciousness, the patronised, starving understudy, waiting for freedom to pronounce its own name.

Revulsion turned to anger as she considered the difference between Athairton and the high-powered capitals of the world. It was human in Athairton. The people were all part of the life of the village, from dear Old Sam to wise Lugh. Each child belonged, participated in a living community, while under the name of progress leaders all over the world flattened the same people into consumer or factory fodder.

She switched off the intruding, alien reflection of life.

A passion mounted inside her that she had never felt before. It was almost male in its aggression. Looking from the window towards the sea, she could see the occasional lights in farm house windows, vulnerable in their isolation. She opened the windows and walked out on to the lawn. The night was still, only a gentle breeze whispered in her ear.

The heady perfume from some wall flowers filled her nostrils. Small animals squeaked and shuffled as they went about their nocturnal business. The passion stretched through her arms and reached for the elements. It soared and returned to her as strength. By Sunday morning she was full of health and energy.

As Lugh had promised her, she had slept soundly all week, waking every morning feeling refreshed and happy. She sorted out a dress that fitted her. It was a green one that she'd once bought but never worn. It was a soft cotton, with long sleeves and a scooped out neckline. It fitted neatly into the waist and then swirled into a flared skirt. It hung on the back of the door, ready for May Day.

Marcus called her from school and asked her to bring him a book on Greek education when she came to stay with Daphne.

"It's on the second shelf down, next to my old Bunter books."

"Have you seen Lugh, Mum?"

"Yes."

"Well, when you see him again, tell him I beat Parkes at chess. I told him I would do it this term." Parkes was the head boy. His exuberance echoed down the phone. She told him about Beltine and the celebrations. He was fascinated and made her promise to tell him all about it.

Before he rang off, something prompted her to ask him what it was that Lugh had told him about his 'Betrothed'. Marcus thought for a while.

"He said something funny. I can't really remember exactly what it was, why?"

"Don't reply to a question with a question," she reminded him. "Think. What exactly did he say?"

"I think she must live abroad."

"Why do you say that?"

"Well, he said something about her not being able to find the way or something. I can't remember anything else, why?"

"I just wondered."

Tufts of green poked out of the soil. The bed of earth, warmed by the sun, was pushing up the new, young vegetables. She wandered round the garden, watching the bees and other insects crawl in and out of the blossom.

Looking across towards Culbone she was suddenly gripped with the mad idea of calling on the mysterious Bridget. An hour later, she was dressed and driving the Lagonda towards the farm with a disgruntled Mac bumping around in the back.

As she walked down the path leading to the farm she began to feel very foolish. What on earth was she doing, running to meet a woman whom she'd never met before. The woman waved.

Isabelle turned to see whether anyone was walking behind her, but no, she was definitely waving to her.

She was sitting on the gate. As Isabelle drew closer she realised that although from a distance Bridget appeared to be about thirty, she was in fact nearer sixty. The hair that had looked so red in the sunlight was, when seen in closer proximity, really quite grey. Her face, although beautiful, was covered in wrinkles. Kind, amber-coloured eyes smiled as she greeted her.

"Mrs. Carrington, I've been expecting you. We'll have lunch together."

It was as if she had known this extraordinary woman all her life. From the moment that she had agreed to have lunch they had talked non-stop.

Bridget recounted wonderful stories about the village, Nodens, and Mrs. Bourama, whose name had also been Brigit. They had been like sisters, she told her.

They had a wholesome lunch, consisting of soup and dark homemade bread. Isabelle could see why the village held Bridget in such reverence. She was wise. Her eyes searched the secret corners of your soul. She seemed to know all about one's life and accepted peoples' contributions as verification of her own understanding.

Her house, like Lugh's, was covered in deerskins. On the walls were pictures of the same symbols and in front of the fire stood a large bronze cauldron. Charts of the universe hung from the walls and over the round central chimney, just above the fire, was an iron pentagram.

After clearing away the earthenware soup bowls, Bridget showed her another room, filled with old books and jars of herbs. There were also ointments, powders and a bunsen burner. It reminded Isabelle of a biology room. "This is where I work," she said. "From this room I can see for miles. Out on the patio there is where I plot the stars' patterns."

What had in the distance looked like sun dials were, in fact, types of chronometers. Isabelle looked round the room. Pieces of paper with scribbled mathematical formulae were scattered everywhere.

"Tomorrow night," she said, sifting through some papers, "is the right time to help you with that worrying dream."

Isabelle was startled. "How did you know about my dream?" she asked.

"We're all going to help you," Bridget replied.

"Tomorrow night, Nuada Finnfail will be at his most powerful, just the right time for Lugh to take you through." She pointed to a chart of the universe.

"Look," she said. "Here is what you would call Neptune. It is lined up with Mars and little Pluto here. Now, we join here and here." She drew a triangle. "And mathematically, everything is perfect for you."

"Who's 'we'?" Isabelle asked suspiciously.

Bridget laughed at her worried expression. "The same party of people who loved and greeted you when you were trapped by the snow. They are all people who care about you. I will be there too, with Morrigan, the vicar."

"But," Isabelle was confused, "isn't it an awful lot of trouble, just for a silly dream?" Bridget looked at her seriously.

"Is it so silly?"

Her eyes bore through the tissue of fear that disguised itself as confused indifference. Isabelle looked at the warmth and love emanating from Bridget's face. "If I had a sister," she blurted, "I'd want her to be like you." Bridget smiled. "You are my sister," she said gently.

The schoolroom was filled with the sound of high-pitched female chatter. As she entered, clutching her white daisies and red anemones, smiling faces greeted her and there were exclamations of delight at the sight of her flowers. Coffee and sandwiches were shared as she joined in the preparations for Beltine.

All the women were threading the flowers together, then laying them in bunches over Lugh's wooden frame until it was completely covered.

Isabelle's daisies were saved for the May Queen's crown. The anemones were all gathered together and tucked into the mound at the top of the wooden bell. Then finally, on top of the anemones, they placed a large china doll, dressed in blue. Garlands of assorted flowers draped her feet.

They sprinkled the whole flowered bell with water and then old Karen came forward and placed a long white veil over the smiling china doll. All the women cheered. They waved to her as she left the hall and promised to see her the following day. Old Karen caught up with her outside.

"Didn't it look beautiful?" she panted. "And when you see the children all dressed up, it makes you feel real spring-like." Lugh was waiting outside in the car. Old Sam waved to her from the back seat. "We'll all see you in a minute," old Karen said, climbing into the front seat.

Isabelle began to feel nervous. They were all driving off as if they were going to a party.

Her hands shook as she turned the ignition.

The pub was emptying. Villagers were making their way home.

She drove carefully up the winding lane home, admonishing herself all the way for allowing such an embarrassing situation.

They were all standing outside the house talking easily amongst themselves while they waited for her. Lugh stepped forward as she approached them and relieved her shaking hands of the front door keys. Gwynneth came and hugged her.

"Did you enjoy making the bell?" she asked. "Wait until tomorrow. The parade starts at eleven. It will look wonderful." They entered the house and Karen bustled forward to turn on the lights.

"Would you like something to drink?" she asked them, feeling like a child going through motions of good behaviour. Bridget took her firmly by the arm and led her into the lounge.

"You are to do nothing, Isabelle. We will do all that there is to be done."

Bridget placed a cushion on the floor for her. She sat on it obediently and watched the activities of the others. Arthur lit a fire. Gwynneth placed four candle sticks in the corners of the room and Karen set up a small altar and covered it with a clean white cloth. The Reverend Morrigan lifted Bridget's cauldron on to the altar and then arranged a sword and a jug of liquid at the side. Mr. Nialls added an ear of corn, Olwen spread a fan, Dermot put a dagger on the altar and Sam placed a loaf of bread in front of the cauldron.

Granya drew the chairs up until they formed a circle.

Maeve arranged some of Bridget's powders near to the fire and Lugh brought in a bowl of water.

Isabelle's heart was pounding. Was Daphne right? Were they witches? What on earth was going to happen?

Bridget entered the room, dressed in a dark blue robe. In her hand she held something that looked like a conductor's baton. Quietly the entire company sat down, except for Lugh, who remained by her side.

Isabelle could hear her own breathing fluttering out of her mouth.

The group was absolutely silent and still. Then, in accord, they began breathing together, as one person.

It sounded as if someone was sleeping very heavily. Soon, she found her own breathing regulated to their timing. Bridget muttered a few words and then all the eyes turned to Isabelle in the centre of the circle.

She felt a small point of warmth centred on her head. Resting her head back on to the cushion behind her, she looked up to see the cause of the heat. A small light was suspended in the air above her. It circled, flashing like a tiny lightouse, reflecting in each pair of eyes seated around the circle.

A faint, high-pitched sound followed, which increased in strength as the circling light grew larger, spinning wildly above her head.

Her head began to feel heavy and her eyes blurred. She was aware of Bridget talking in a strange language. Flames sprang from the cauldron.

Then came the silence. It was so great that her ears felt like a receiver for all the sound waves in the world. The weight and enormity of it pinned her to the floor.

Out of the blue blackness Lugh's face appeared, lit by the spinning light.

He whispered in her ear, "Trust me". The echoing words spun through the hollow chambers of her brain. She felt her heavy head lifted, as he placed his arm around her. His musky smell crept through to her consciousness. The dark tunnel opened up and she fell, silently screaming, as she rushed faster and faster, through twisting, squeezing blackness, until the pinprick of light appeared. The arms held her as she travelled. The sound of "Trust me" penetrated the tunnel and pushed her faster towards the growing brightness.

Blinding light filled her eyes. It was like an exploding sun. Then she was through, drifting in a world of blue sky and pure air.

As she breathed, she soared upwards, luxuriating in the space around her.

"COME DOWN."

"Yes," she answered, without speaking.

The child was there. She was sitting among the grazing cows, her head bowed in concentration.

"CAN YOU SEE HER?"

"Yes."

"CALL HER."

She called the child. The little head lifted. The wind tugged at her hair.

She called again.

The child stood up and listened. Then slowly she turned and looked in the direction of the sound.

It was Isabelle Cullen, smiling at her and raising a small arm in welcome.

Then she fell, fast towards her, like an arrow towards a mark. Blackness.

She saw the world of a nine year old. The cows munched loudly. They were huge animals whose eyes challenged her.

A droning sound came from the sky. She looked up. They came like black dots in the distance.

Smoke was coming up from the ground. It was in the direction where she and Mummy went shopping. There were loud bump noises.

He was there, running towards her. She wondered whether he would recognise her immediately.

There was the familiar musky smell as he lifted her into his arms.

"Come on, darling. The Germans are coming."

He hadn't known her.

Quickly, he carried her across the fields as the bumps came closer. Into the shelter. Dark with whispered voices of shadowy neighbours.

Sitting on his knee.

Turn to him and let him know who it is.

His eyes, dark blue, smile at her.

She puts her child's arms around his neck.

Can he see behind this shell?

He sees and recognises her. His eyes glint in the torchlight. His arms tighten.

She can only use the child's voice to express herself.

"I'll love you forever," she whispers.

Blackness overwhelms her.

"WHAT IS THE MATTER?"

"I'm lost."

"ARE YOU STILL WITH ISABELLE?"

"I'm losing her."

His eyes are watching her, but she can't talk.

There are green walls and bustling women called nurses. Bars are on her bed, through which she can see a big door.

If she wanted to open it to go home she would not be able to reach the handle.

He is crying. The man standing near him, with a moustache, is a doctor.

I am leaving this shell.

She is in space again, looking down to where he sits with the sick child.

"I'm losing you," she shouts to him, beating the air.

He reaches for the child's small hand.

Isabelle Cullen opens her eyes.

Panic.

I have no home now. I must drift.

"LET THE TIME PASS."

Blackness, drifting, waiting.

"They are together by the gate."

"GO TO HER."

"I don't want to, I want to stay with him."

"YOU CAN'T! YOU MUST LIVE HER LIFE."

"No."

"TRUST ME."

The child is about twelve and dressed in a uniform. She calls her as the bell sounds inside the convent.

The child Isabelle turns, she has fear in her eyes. She falls fast towards her.

The taste of fear hits her. It is disgusting and not for her. She reaches for his hand and looks at him.

His eyes understand that she has returned.

A nun comes to lead her away. She doesn't want to go. He walks towards the gate, then turns back to wave to her.

He says he will see her at Easter.

On her knees. Many girls on their knees, chanting about unknown sins. The nun stares at her. She can see her inside the shell.

She thinks like Isabelle and fears the nuns, but at night she escapes from the suffocating atmosphere inside the convent. She leaves the shell and tries to reach him.

"WHAT IS YOUR NAME?"

"Erinna. Brigantia."

"ARE YOU TWO?"

"No, just me, Erinna. Yes, I must come here."

The nun is approaching. She is calling Isabelle to her study. He is dead. His plane has been shot down.

Blackness.

"WHERE ARE YOU?"

"Isabelle has fainted and I want to leave. I can't leave, I must fulfil the destiny."

"IS THAT ERINNA OR BRIGANTIA?"

"It is I, Erinna, I want to be born again, where he and I can be together."

"WHERE IS BRIGANTIA?"

"I am here, I must stay, but Erinna is weakening me."

"YOU MUST FUSE WITH ERINNA."

"No. I will try. No, I will suspend until I find him. But that will weaken me, Brigantia."

"YOU MUST BOTH STAY. LET TIME PASS, ERINNA."

Blackness.

"I have found him."

"ERINNA?"

"Lugh, I have found you. You have a shell that is twelve years younger than this one."

"YES, ERINNA. I AM HERE, BUT YOU MUST FUSE WITH BRIGANTIA."

"No, I want you for myself."

"YOU ARE DEFYING DAGDA. YOU KNOW THERE IS A REASON FOR ALL THINGS."

"I can't get back, Lugh, I'm drifting. Help me Brigantia."

"ERINNA? NUADA IS PASSING. LET TIME PASS UNTIL MY DAY, THEN WE WILL HELP YOU."

The gentle clucks from the hens penetrated Isabelle's deep slumber. As she turned, she became aware of Lugh's arm around her. Where was she?

Of course, the strange ritual. She must have fallen asleep. Lugh would naturally have stayed to see that she was all right.

A slight beard had grown around his chin. The new rays of sunshine accentuated his profile, creating a light around his face that gave an illusion of a golden god. He opened his eyes.

"Good morning," he smiled sleepily. "How are you feeling now?"

Kneeling and looking down at him, she knew that any words were unnecessary. He understood how she felt.

A sense of purpose, warmth and energy. A feeling of life.

"What happened, Lugh? Why do I feel so alive?"

"Bridget conducted a healing ceremony for you, you will have no more dreams now."

It felt so natural, cooking breakfast for him and talking together so easily about the day's celebrations. Words tumbled out, as if she was trying to catch up with a life-time's sharing. After he had left for the village, the strength remained, so that she charged about the house completing her chores.

Changed into fresh clothes, she set off to the village, to see the start of the procession. As she walked there, she felt that she'd grown about six inches in height. She felt strong and fit.

When she joined the crowd waiting for the procession she was completely at ease and greeted the smiling faces warmly. There was no fear of them, only a sense of protection. A strength to defend them and the Athairton way of life. A slow drumbeat came from the direction of the school.

A little boy appeared. He was dressed in white and solemnly carried a flag. He followed Old Sam who was leading the procession and banging the drum.

Behind them, two other children, covered in garlands, walked slowly as they played their small whistles. Following these two were a couple of children dressed as King and Queen. They walked sedately by, leading a trail of other boys and girls who were dressed as footmen and maids of honour, or lords and ladies.

At the end of the procession walked a child dressed in the same type of robe that Bridget had worn during the previous night's ceremony. Behind her a small boy followed, dressed in deerskins and carrying a spear.

With their ribbons and veils floating in the slight breeze, they marched through the village towards the old oak by the Tuatha Arms. There on the small green stood a colourful maypole.

She felt someone squeeze her arm. It was Bridget.

"Hello, sister," she said.

They linked arms and followed the marching children.

"These are your people," Bridget said to her as they walked. "Our people, to be defended forever."

The May Queen was chosen. A lovely child with long fair hair. Bridget placed the crown of daisies on her beautiful head. Then came the Maypole dancing, accompanied by singing and laughter.

Round the maypole, trit, trit, trot.
See what a maypole, we have got,
Fine and gay
Trip away
Happy is our new May Day.

The men from the village performed the Morris dancing and then everyone was running to the large paddock where the deer was slowly cooking on the barbecue.

As the people ate and drank various cider cups a play was enacted about Robin Hood and Maid Marion.

After the play everyone joined in the games.

Walking home back up the hill Isabelle saw the glowing bonfires dotted on the hillside. Bellowing cattle were being herded around them by the dancing villagers. From the woods shrieks of glee reverberated as the children played hide and seek in the remaining daylight.

Looking at her youthful reflection in the full length mirror Isabelle marvelled at her own appearance. She appeared flushed and almost virginal.

If Daphne could see her now, she thought, she would immediately suspect her of having had a face lift.

Her reflection in the mirror showed a woman who looked more like thirty-eight instead of forty-eight. As she twirled and preened, delighting in her own femininity, she realised that the convent-inspired guilt for any form of sensuality had been banished forever.

Lugh called for her at eight o'clock.

As she opened the door to him, she felt as excited as a young girl on her first date. She was breathless as she greeted him. Carefully, he fastened the necklace of seashells around her neck. He then placed a shell in the shape of a ring on the fourth finger of her right hand.

"I feel like a mermaid," she laughed.

The doors were closed. The village hall was silent although the lights were blazing inside. Isabelle looked at Lugh.

"Are you sure there's a dance here?" she asked him.

"Ssh," he said. "Wait now."

He knocked three times on the hall door.

O'Leary's voice boomed out. "Is that the sun rising in the west? Might it be Samildanach?"

"It is," Lugh shouted.

The doors were flung open, music played and they were grabbed by the waiting people. She could never in her life remember dancing so hectically.

There were endless reels and formation dancing. The whole night was full of laughter and gaiety. The last dance was a waltz.

Lugh held her gently and guided her carefully through the milling couples on the hot dance floor.

As they danced with light, weaving movements, she could feel the pressure of his palm on the base of her spine. Heat pulsed through her veins and electricity coursed through her body towards his hand. Her new strength rejected any warnings from her old personality. Instead, she drew nearer, revelling in the warmth of his being.

They walked to her front door, hand in hand and talking about the evening's fun. "Your first Beltine of many".

"Thank you, Lugh."

"It was my pleasure." He smiled.

His eyes seemed to be searching her own. Slowly, he took her face into his hands.

The gentleness of his lips was like the softness of velvet, yet the desire it created was like the pull from the moon to the sea.

The passion was strengthened by denial.

Gently, he said goodnight to her and after reminding her to be careful when she drove to Brighton, he walked away.

As she lay out the shells on the dressing table that night she knew that she was experiencing the love that she had thought only existed in dreams.

CHAPTER NINE

The old hen squawked in protest as Isabelle pushed her broody feathery body aside to reach for the warm eggs. Three hens had become broody in the last week.

Pecking furiously at her hand the brown hen turned to glare at her with her small red rimmed eyes. "All right," Isabelle crooned. "Keep your eggs."

The sun warmed her shoulders as she crouched and felt under the nesting boxes. Two white hens had started hiding their eggs there. A trail of feathers and droppings had led her to their secret nest.

Mac watched wistfully from outside the run as she collected more eggs for Daphne. Boiled eggs were her favourite breakfast, especially the ones from Nodens, and Isabelle intended that she should have enough for supper as well.

The vegetables were pushing further out of the ground. So was the parsley. Its feathery leaves reached towards the sunshine.

She dug some rhubarb for Daphne.

The predatory birds that hovered over the kitchen garden looking for the young shoots were frightened off by Sam's flapping scarecrow and some blood-red painted bottles that he'd placed upside down in the soil. "They'll think it's their friends with their heads chopped off," he told her, glaring at the pigeons and crows that were pacing along the fence.

He was fixing the cage for the raspberries and gooseberries.

"These are Lord Derbys, Isabelle, them's the pink fat uns, they won't prickle yer mouth like the others," he said, lovingly fondling the gooseberry foliage.

"Yes, I can promise you, you'll have gooseberry tart for shick shack day."

"What's that?" she said. "It sounds terrible."

"You don't know shick shack day?" he said, horrified at her ignorance.

"No." She shook her head, laughing at the expression of horror.

"Well, on shick shack day, you'd better wear an oak leaf, 'cause if you don't they'll call you a jick jack."

"What's a jick jack?"

"Someone who isn't noticed, a nothing, I think. It's rude, I know that much, so don't let them call you no jick jack, get yourself some oak leaves that day."

The greenhouse was full of small vulnerable tomato and cucumber plants. Isabelle chose six tomato plants for Daphne and thought about Old Sam's jick jack. She hadn't existed before. Even her son had noticed her fading into insignificance whenever confronted by people.

Why had she been like that?

Was it the loss of her father, when she was twelve?

But other girls lost their fathers in the war and they had emerged stronger, more self reliant. Was it the convent? The nuns with their sick emphasis on guilt and subservience? But other girls had survived. One had even hit Sister Mary Helen in the face.

The first of the teacher bashers, she thought wryly.

She sat by the pool in the walled garden and wondered about Mrs. Bourama. Had she ever been insignificant?

Frog spawn clung to the water lilies. An occasional beetle created a tiny wash as it scudded across the water.

Was it the boarding house that had created her sense of inferiority? Memories of her over-anxious mother turning the beautiful house into a boarding house after her father's death crept into her consciousness. Embarrassing holidays, her bedroom the small attic so that her mother could squash the uncouth holiday makers into every available room. Not being able to ask her friends to the house in the summer.

"Don't tell your friends I'm letting rooms, dear, they might think we've come down in the world." Why had she been like that?

As she looked into the pool her mother's voice echoed in her memory. "Of course you must marry Chris Carrington. His family are so rich and respectable. You'll never have to slave like me."

She felt anger.

What a waste of precious time, all that jick jacking.

She felt loath to leave Nodens, even for the few days that she was going to stay with Daphne. The act of packing seemed a betrayal.

She had moaned about returning to Brighton to Bridget, over coffee. "No, you must go," she said firmly. "It will do you good. It will clarify things for you."

"All that way to vote," Isabelle had groaned.

"Well I can tell you, the woman will be Prime Minister, but you must still go."

"How do you know?" Isabelle asked. All the polls had indicated that it would be a very close fight and Chris was sure that she wouldn't win.

"The time has come for the woman," she laughed. "It's all in the stars, Isabelle." As they walked to the gate Bridget told her that when she returned from Brighton she would start teaching her all that she knew. "It's time I think," she had said.

The weather remained fine for her journey on the fourth.

Mac's tail drooped when he saw the cases and his dog bowl being loaded into the car. He promptly ran off and hid in the bushes by the side of the hen house.

As she drove across the moors she saw the bright yellow gorse and soft purple heather dotted over the hills. Winding her way through the Quantocks she looked up at the trees, standing stately and proud, their varied green hues vivid against the pale blue skyline. Their glistening leaves shook with numbers of cavorting birds.

Leaving Somerset, empty spaces appeared by the roadside. Spaces where old buildings had once stood. Weeds grew among abandoned, rusting machines. Shining office blocks that hid anonymous workers behind tinted windows assaulted her sensibilities.

Stark, dead-looking, giant blocks of flats towered bleakly over smaller prefabs, the only sign of human life there being the occasional, fluttering grey washing.

As she passed through each town she saw suspicious people, locking their cars and clutching their purses fearfully, while their darting eyes searched passers-by for the slightest hint of aggression.

Every main street had long bus queues of sad-faced people. Cocooned inside the Lagonda, Isabelle watched the passing show of human life. She felt as if she had just woken up after a thirty year sleep.

"What happened to us?" she thought. "How did England change so badly after the war? How was it possible to smash the environment, instil such hostility and fear into people so that they became blank-faced zombies?" Brighton was dirty. Filthy paper tissues clung to peeling iron railings that were protected by the National Trust. Weeds grew on the pavements that were a parking ground for dogs' excreta.

Driving past the labour exchange, she saw a long queue. Greasy-haired youths stood by girls with drooping hemlines. Bewildered middle-aged men attempted to retain some smartness by brushing the dandruff from their shoulders.

A rage grew inside Isabelle. What had happened to reduce the people of Britain, a noble people, to this shuffling apology with no human dignity?

Tory stickers decorated Daphne's windows. On the opposite side of the street red posters offered an alternative. All the smiling poster faces promised to give the people more and raise standards. "To what?" she growled. "To more suspicion and isolation. To bigger buildings that reduce man's physical stature to that of an ant?"

Daphne hugged her. Then, after unpacking all the eggs and plants, turned and looked at her in amazement.

"You've lost more weight. My God, Isabelle, you must be a size ten." She scowled. "I've only lost four pounds on my Weight Watchers."

Inviting smells came from the kitchen. A large dish of lasagne was plonked on to the table. "But Daphne, if you eat lasagne, of course you're not going to lose weight."

Between laughter, they fell over each other's words in a noisy gabble, each one trying to inform the other of her news.

Daphne had met a new man at a Conservative party meeting. "Darling, he's something to do with watches or something. He drives a Mercedes and, believe it or not, he's actually single. The only thing is, I'll have to learn to play golf." Isabelle laughed at the idea of Daphne trudging around a golf course after the unsuspecting man.

She told Daphne about Beltine and the May Day celebrations but left out anything about the ritual for healing her dream. The fact was that she didn't really know what had happened. All she could remember was the spinning light and falling asleep. She didn't want to tell Daphne about waking up beside Lugh in case she made a joke about it. Her friendship with Lugh was too precious to be spoilt by cheap remarks.

How lovely it was to explore another woman's dressing table. Daphne had bought some new make-up and the man with the watches had bought her some new perfume. The two women spent a blissful hour trying different coloured creams with the same enjoyment as a couple of children with a new paintbox.

After a boiled egg supper with Emma the two women curled up in dressing gowns to watch the last of the party political broadcasts before the election. After the news, Isabelle launched into an attack on the way the people of the country had lost their spirit.

Daphne looked at her in amazement. "Something's happened to you," she said. "It's as if you were another person. I've never known you to be so . . ." She paused, searching for a definition.

"Please don't take this as an insult, but you've never really had so much strength, yes, that's it. You've never felt strongly about anything before."

Isabelle listened to her, watching her reactions.

Yes, she had changed and her relationship with Daphne had altered accordingly. Although she still enjoyed the feminine prattling and superficial chatter there had been some uneasy moments when she felt bored with regurgitated subjects. Also a few of Daphne's attitudes which in the past had always amused her had caused her to feel a mild irritation, which surprised her.

She knew that now, she was stronger than Daphne. An almost masculine tolerance of Daphne's selfish materialism permitted her to feel some humour over her confidences, but her disparaging remarks about her friends forced Isabelle into the sad acceptance that she had nearly outgrown a friendship.

The guest bedroom was a glorious tribute to Laura Ashley, with lace-covered cushions and pieces of Wedgwood scattered around the room. The drive had tired her. Thankfully, she sank between pretty, feminine sheets and relaxed under the electric over-blanket.

Drunks staggered up the little street, shouting football cheers to remembered matches.

Police sirens wailed and bored youths revved their motor bikes.

May the fifth was announced loudly over a microphone as active party workers drove down the Brighton streets, urging people to vote.

Breakfast was supervised by an energetic Daphne, sporting a blue rosette. Knockers were out in the street, smiling politely and offering usually isolated old ladies conversation and transport in exchange for their valuable vote. Polling stations were filled with glassy-eyed party workers, improvising tales of horror in the event of the other 'lot' getting in.

Hysteria was everywhere except for the Librium-calmed women who stood smiling like retarded saints. Isabelle approached the voting booth.

Bridget had said that the woman would be the next Prime Minister.

As she looked at the list of names offered, revolutionary thoughts almost forced her to tear up the voting slip but as always, she placed her cross and folded the cheap paper. The bored teller was intent on exploring the wonders of earwax, so ignored her as she posted her slip.

As Daphne was totally involved in her election activities Isabelle called on the McAnallys and took a last look at the house in Clifton Villas.

The flowering cherry was in full bloom and the forsythia spread along the railings. A quick moment of nostalgia and regret for all the sad moments past, then she was free, a stranger, looking back in time. Her roots were now in Athairton.

The McAnallys, like so many intellectual Socialists, were in a quandry. Sadness accompanied their decision to vote Liberal. Kind, gentle people, they were confused as their ideals and dreams of Utopia faded with society's contrary behaviour. Books were discussed and themes from the latest plays appearing at the Theatre Royal before going to the West End.

Isabelle told them about Athairton. She wanted them to share the experience of life in the village so promises of holidays were made, subject to lecture tours.

She sat with Daphne watching the television and burping from the fish and chips supper. Long into the night they listened to the pundits, until they staggered wearily to bed. Bridget's predictions turned out to be true. The country, exhausted after the frenzied elections, heaved a sigh and hoped for miracles.

Next morning Isabelle bought some dresses, had her hair done, and then called into Hurstwood to see Marcus.

After checking to see that she'd brought the right book for his project they drove to the village tea-rooms.

Marcus ate platefuls of cakes and between mouthfuls told her about the school elections. "Who won?" she asked him. "Who do you think?" he replied sourly. "The blinking Tories."

"Who did you vote for?" she asked, watching him wipe his sticky fingers on his trousers. "The Friends of the Earth, of course. What's the point of any party getting in if they're going to pollute us out of existence," he said angrily.

She reached out and hugged him. He cared. He cared as she did for the land and the people.

She looked at his cheeky face which was scrutinising her appearance.

"You're looking awfully good, you know Mum. Years younger."

She told him about Beltine and the rest of the news from the village. "I wish I'd been there. Still when I'm a farmer I'll be part of it all then."

The familiar ache returned as she drove him back to school.

"Lugh sent me a painting of Nodens, Mum, to remind me," he said.

He looked at her inquisitively.

"Have you heard from Dad?"

"No," she replied.

"Neither have I," he said. "It was kind of Lugh to think of me, wasn't it?"

"Yes," she said, with indiscreet warmth.

His alert ears caught the change in sound and he smiled knowingly.

Mac had a romp around the school grounds before she left. Sneakily, she and Marcus bundled him back into the car, hoping that no-one would associate them with the lone turd in the middle of the cricket pitch.

She drove as fast as she could on the way back to Nodens. The days' impressions flickered through her mind like the shapes of the passing houses. Daphne and her superficial chattering. The decay in all the towns. The prejudiced inanities, spoken in the hairdressers. The deadness of so-called civilization. What was happening?

Brigantia stirred. Her awareness and knowledge, that stretched back for thousands of years, forced its way into Isabelle's thinking and created a second's flash of understanding. A brief glimpse of the truth.

It was systems that killed the people. Ever since the Romans had imposed their bureaucracy across Britain, it had grown like a creeping fungus, killing the free souls of Britons. Whatever name you called the system, it destroyed the spirit of the people.

"What good," she raged, as she drove the car furiously, "is it to overproduce food, so that it has to be thrown away, when there are people starving? Why do all these people shout about equality, when there is a pecking order even among chickens? Why do some people want everyone to be the same, when their very differences give colour and meaning to the world? Why produce more cars, when the world is running out of oil? Systems," she yelled, "systems destroyed the conscience of the people.

"Systems destroyed that conscience that elected the right word to be spoken. The word came to the conscience from the universal conscience and was spoken by people who did not seek power or control but were content to be an individual part of the community."

Tears streamed down her face as Brigantia shared with her the endless battles for free spirits through the ages.

No wonder that Bridget had told her that things would be clarified. She knew now that her destiny was to protect Athairton. The little Eden, where each villager was in harmony with the way of life.

The wise and strong leading, helping the others, yet always aware that they were only a part of the living conscience of the village. They didn't control or want power, they were content for each soul to have moments of glory and they loved them for it.

It was late when she drove through Athairton. Apart from a light glimmering in Lugh's cottage, the whole village was asleep.

The stars sparkled down from the cool dark night.

Parking the car quietly, she groped her way along the stone steps towards his gate. As she opened the gate, a hedgehog cried like a child in the darkness. She stopped and listened to it shuffling about in the garden. A sheep started coughing in the field next to the cottage as she made her way to the porch.

His face was smudged with paint.

"Welcome home," he said, hugging her. She clung to him, breathing in deeply the wonderful smell of his skin and paint-covered jumper. The smell of wholesome man.

Over cocoa, she told him about her new thoughts. He listened intently to all she had to say.

"Quite soon, you will know more," he said.

His face lit up when she told him how much Marcus had appreciated his painting.

"I want him to love his home." he said.

She opened her bedroom window and breathed in the perfumed air. The huge expanse of starry sky curved round her, filling her spirit with a sense of wonder.

Distant lights twinkling far out at sea reminded her of the tiny spark of man's existence in the vast universe.

The white hawthorns blazed from the hedges. Swallows nested. Sam planted the runner beans. Then the rain poured down from the skies, plastering the blossom into the ground. The chickens huddled inside their nesting boxes. Even the young cockerel lost his jauntiness. Fires continued to be lit while curtains were sewn and household duties carried on.

Old Karen moaned to Isabelle about her arthritis. "I'll have to have a go at those old bees again," she muttered as she polished the lounge. A bedraggled magpie pecked at the window and Isabelle undid the latch to let him inside.

"Don't let him in!" shrieked Karen.

It was too late. The wet bird hopped on to the sill and shook its feathers, staring malevolently at Karen who was shouting and waving her duster at him.

Isabelle couldn't believe the pantomime that followed. Karen charged at the magpie, shouting and flapping her duster. The bird immediately scuttled under Chris' favourite armchair. There was a wail and a curse from Karen who proceeded to shake the chair like someone possessed. The magpie scuttled into the hall, followed by Karen shoo-shooing. There was a loud slam of the front door as Karen chased the bird outside.

"Are you all right Karen?" Isabelle asked, thinking that the old woman might be having a fit.

She was sitting on a kitchen chair, muttering and swinging a small muslin bag around her in which there appeared to be a selection of herbs. She looked up to Isabelle and sighed.

"Please dear, don't ever let a tapping bird into the house again. It's not a good omen."

She hobbled back into the lounge.

"Nasty old devil," she muttered.

Blissful days were spent with Bridget as the teaching began. Old star maps were laid out for her to study and she was told about the ancient giant map, built into the earth around the Tor at Glastonbury. She studied the sun and its effects on earth according to its position with respect to the mid-heaven.

The moon, she learned, by its proximity to earth, could change everything according to her light. The stars too, whether fixed or moveable, were the cause of vibrations, influencing life on earth. As the days warmed, she became more engrossed with the alpha and omega of the universal mystery. Old Sam helped her studies by explaining the effects on plants from the moon at her quarters and syzygies.

"I don't know all that Bridget knows, mind. She usually tells us things in advance, but I do know that there are natural relations in plants. Take the runner beans for instance. He hates to be planted near the onions." He shook his head. "If he's planted near the onions he droops and mopes, but if you plant him near sweet peas he's happy as anything."

Shick shack day came and she decked the house with oak branches and following Sam's advice wore an oak leaf. Never again would she ever allow herself to be a nothing jick jack.

The gooseberries were miraculously fat and pink and she made the earliest gooseberry pies that she'd ever cooked. Lugh and Arthur had been out to sea and caught some large crabs. Karen and Bridget came over and helped her to prepare the food. With asparagus from the garden, Gwynneth's parsley soup and Bridget's mint ice-cream, the Athairtons gorged themselves at Nodens' first shick shack supper.

While the others sang to Dermot's guitar Lugh and Isabelle stood in the garden and Lugh explained to her the reality of Bridget's old star map by pointing to them in the heavens.

"There's the golden fleece of Aries looking towards the old bull Taurus who's threatening the twins, Gemini. Next to them is the crab, Cancer, who's cross I should think with my star Leo, the lion, for catching some of his earthly family."

Isabelle laughed, "Thank you lion, they were delicious."

"Virgo, the virgin, stands next to the roaring lion and tames him with her gentleness." "Virgo's my sign," she interrupted.

"I know," he replied.

"Libra," he went on, "balances life next to her and over there," he turned her towards the other direction and held her to him while he pointed out the stars, "there is Andromeda, five different stars. She's wondering whether Perseus there has the strength and constancy to reach her."

"And does he?" she asked, holding his hand.

"Yes," he replied, kissing her on the forehead.

She watched the skylark rising straight up into the clear blue sky. Her eyes squinted in the bright sunshine. Though she was tired after being woken by the insane cockerel crowing in the middle of the night she was sun-tanned and happy. Fat green swellings clustered in the orchard as the apples and pears basked in the sun's warmth. Cherries, too, glowed amongst the leaves.

Bridget was coming over later to show her dowsing. With any luck she could find the well that Chris wanted. As she walked towards the summer house she looked for his yew tree. She was sure that he'd planted it somewhere nearby.

It was lying on the ground. But it had seemed so healthy when he'd planted it. She looked for the cause of the small tree's death.

Moles. Their burrowing had uprooted the small tree.

It was a hazel twig in the shape of an inverted Y and about a foot long.

"Now, hold your palm upwards and clench your fist firmly round the ends," Bridget advised her. "Point the single end of the twig forward and parallel with the ground."

Isabelle moved slowly, watching the twig for signs of movement. It twitched. "Oh," she yelped.

Giggling stupidly, she watched the twig pulling towards the ground.

"There's enough water there for a well, I should think."

Bridget chuckled and held the twig herself for confirmation. It waggled comically, setting Isabelle off into fresh paroxysms of laughter.

June was all the colours in the world poured into the garden. Looking as brown as a berry Isabelle spent her days gardening, bottling fruit and making pounds of jam.

The lessons with Bridget continued, turning their friendship into perfect unity as they studied together, herbs, the tree of life, sounds and colours. She felt as free as a child with the world open for discovery. Her sense of smell, colour and sound heightened as she greeted each new day with wonder.

When the phone call came, it shocked her into numbness.

It was from Yehedi. He spoke softly, his voice shaking with emotion.

Chris had gone over to Iran to safeguard a client's interests. There had been an outbreak of mob violence and he had been caught in some cross-fire.

They were flying his body back to England.

CHAPTER TEN

The tears were tears of regret.

Regret that Chris should have instigated the move to Nodens and yet not shared the life that she had discovered. Regret that her inner feelings had been locked in the exile of her subconscious and regret that he had never sought nor shared them. From their very first encounter they had behaved towards each other in manners dictated by their own environmental systems. His had been a rigidly polite one.

During his childhood his parents had communicated with him from a genteel distance.

"I didn't realise women farted," he had commented when, relaxed after a party, she had let rip in the kitchen. His expression of shock guaranteed failure for any basic humour in the marriage.

The partnership had been based on a series of observed incidents rather than participation. They had stayed together out of good manners.

His tough public school background prevented any show of emotion other than patriotism and musical appreciation. With Marcus, he could manage a fatherly pat on the shoulder but when confronted with her tactile, loving relationship with their son he would retreat with embarrassment from such 'sloppiness'.

Sex to Chris had been a great effort not to let the side down. A physical feat to be performed in a series of quick, silent press ups, with a shower afterwards, to wash away the guilt. Isabelle's inhibitions and inexperience hadn't helped. Brainwashed in the convent against all sensual pleasure. Threatened by venial and mortal sins during adolescence, she had been trapped into rigid conformity. Chris' unease over sex had confirmed her feelings of rejection. That her body was indeed the dirty, fallen dust from which she had to be redeemed.

The traffic roared past as she walked down Throgmorton Street. Appropriately dressed in black wool she perspired in the humid atmosphere. Her nylon tights wrinkled in the heat and some grit from demolition work in the road flew into her eye, which heightened the appearance of mourning when she walked into the solicitor's office.

She picked up a Country Life from the investment pamphlets on the table, poking at her eye from behind the pages. The second generation West Indian telephonist-come-receptionist surveyed her with cold-eyed indifference. Rural scenes swam before her eyes. Sotheby's valuable auctions reminded her of the ghastly auction of her mother's house and Chris' proffered handkerchief, "Come on Bumble, pull yourself together." How she regretted being unable to help him.

Because of the inferiority complex imposed on her by her anxious mother and the abject subservience drummed into her by the convent she had been to Chris as a dried sponge is to a deserted lonely beach. Blown hither and thither across the lifeless pebbles of his social world.

Inside the office there were gentle murmurs of quiet understanding. Of course Chris had arranged everything neatly and tidily, right down to the smaller bequests. That was the sort of man he had been. Even his own death had been thought out carefully.

He was to be cremated, then placed under a tree at Nodens.

She queried the up-to-date will and was told that he'd anticipated trouble in the Middle East so revised it in March. Trusts were explained, papers were signed, and all funeral arrangements would be made by them.

A taxi was called and she was placed inside with more comforting words. She waited until the taxi turned the corner before lighting a cigarette.

There was a solid traffic jam along Park Lane. As the taxi man ranted about the social security scroungers, the Arabs, and the price of petrol, Isabelle half listened and watched the passers-by.

She considered what it was to be the bereaved in the drama of death. She was aware that she merged like a chameleon with the reactions of others.

She thought of David, who had naturally been distraught when she had told him. Gratefully she had soaked up his anguish relieved to feel something after the initial numbness. The Athairtonians comforted her with their philosophical acceptance, talking with her tirelessly until her strength returned. They shared stories of their own past bereavements with her. Sam saw death as only a part of the whole existence, as with the plants. Old Karen, after she'd thumped the table and blamed the magpie for being responsible for the death, told a funny story about a death in the village. During a wake, it seemed, the corpse had twitched, sending the whole gathering shrieking into the street.

She had talked long into the night with Bridget. Her advice was to warn her of the dangers of self-pity and regret. "Don't return to another prison," she told her. "Jump back into the stream of life. You'll miss it if you cling with remorse to the weeds on the bank."

Victoria Station was chaotic and filthy. Student hitch-hikers wandered around with their bulky packs. Horrified tourists arrived from Gatwick to be confronted by spitting down-and-outs among the teeming squalor. The police moved ineffectually amongst the pushing crowds. Wailing babies were carted through jostling people to a day by the ozone and flushed toddlers yowled as they returned, burnt from the sun. Their pleas to be lifted were brushed aside by their tiddly adolescent parents.

Daphne was going to meet her at Brighton.

She sat among the rolling beer cans, orange peel and other debris in the carriage and remembered Chris' warnings about the decline in England. An old couple sat opposite her, their modest luggage arranged neatly on the rack above. Conspicuous in their cleanliness, they clung together like pioneers among unfriendly natives. Lost-looking Englishmen in shabby suits gazed at babbling foreigners decked in expensive clothes and sporting heavy gold chains. Aggressive youths of indeterminate sex sullenly sipped from cans of beer then squeezed their hatred out of them. They placed their dusty feet up on to the seats opposite, toyed with the bent tins and willed their fellow travellers to object.

She arrived at Brighton.

Daphne's cheerful chatter soothed the tensions caused by the journey.

As they turned into the little street to Daphne's house they were confronted by the sight of large-bellied old men wandering in the direction of the sea. Resplendent in their shorts, their burnt bodies angrily pink, they waddled on chubby varicose-veined legs. "Why do they take their clothes off?" Daphne shrieked. "From now until September I shall be treated to daily doses of the British at large, right outside my window." The headmaster had advised her not to tell Marcus until after the final 'O' level, so she passed the few days with Daphne, swimming, telling the few close friends about Chris' death and planning her life.

This form of civilised life was definitely not for her. It was empty and full of decay. Her future was in Athairton. Sharing the old customs and healthy attitudes of true British community or, as the villagers insisted, Celtic tradition. She wanted Marcus to live there. To live a life of maturing wisdom, not to get caught up with the warped fashionable philosophies of the 'with it' cities, changing every year to accommodate the ramblings spawned by trendy cult figures. There was no real loneliness in Athairton.

Amongst the overbright social gatherings that she attended with Daphne isolation screamed from behind smiling masks.

Marcus took the news calmly.

"You know, he was like a Greek," he declared. "Like one of the Spartans." They walked through the college grounds, hand in hand, giving comfort to each other.

"Let's plant an ash for him," he said. "He would have liked that, don't you think, Mum?"

"The oak and the ash?" Isabelle smiled. "Yes, he would have approved of that."

She watched him pack his clothes. There were only another three weeks before the holidays. "It's better," the housemaster had agreed, "that he return home with you now, Mrs. Carrington."

She looked round the stark ambience of the dormitory. Home snapshots vied for predominance against posters and lurid nudes. How could flabby-faced Members of Parliament, sheltered by officialdom, work themselves into such a lather over this so-called privilege? To stir up more ill-informed envy and resentment, she supposed.

The Lagonda pulled hard towards Somerset. They sat silently most of the way, both wrapped up in their own thoughts. She caught sight of a tear trickling down his face and heard the sound of noisy aggressive nose blowing. "Don't be ashamed to cry," she blurted out, her own eyes filling in sympathy. "It isn't manly not to cry about things that move you, whatever the damned system says. It's manly to show your feelings. It proves you're a true human being."

His voice, hampered by a pubescent break, struggled to articulate between sobs.

"He wasn't allowed to be human, was he, Mum? He was brought up like the Spartans." As his mind sought a thread for his theory his sobs died away to be replaced by sniffs and gulps.

"When I was working on the Greeks, I thought, they had to have discipline to have obedient soldiers, the same with the Romans. But when they had bad leaders, then it all fell apart. Is that what Dad meant do you think? When he said that bureaucrats were killing England?" They both considered the theory.

She was bewildered that he could have been following the same train of thought as her own. It was strange. Had he been as influenced by Nodens and the Athairton way of life as she had been?

"You see," he went on searching for words, "it's not real discipline, is it? I mean, doing something because you know it's to be done, it's because you're frightened. It's . . ." He paused.

"It's an enforced, inhuman system," Isabelle yelled. Marcus cheered her statement. Rebellious vigour filled their hearts as the car spent towards Nodens.

Only David and June had been expected to attend the simple ceremony. Marcus spotted the group of dark-suited men. They approached Isabelle in a reverent file. After announcing their respective companies, they added their deepest sympathies. As the curtain fell on his last appearance, the purifying flames turned Chris Carrington's body into dust. The dark-suited men melted away.

Arthur O'Leary had found a proud young ash.

Silently, the Carringtons planted it over the precious dust. They stood in a group, a few yards from the summer house, their heads bowed in memory. Across the fields of ripening corn drifted the scents of rich spicy grass mingled with jasmine. Orchards sighed with the weight of ripening fruit and cattle and sheep grazed contentedly.

Chris was at rest in perfect England.

Bridget had arranged a party at her home. The Athairtons gathered the Carringtons into the warmth of their hearts and sang them songs about life and rebirth, saluting Chris in a wonderful wake. David and June relaxed, grateful for the delicious food, music and shared friendship.

Marcus' and Isabelle's future was discussed, with David honouring his brother's last wishes by educating them further about self-sufficiency. There was enough money to educate Marcus and some capital left in trust for when he was eighteen.

Money from the sale of Clifton Villas, and some insurance policies, left Isabelle with an income that would have been modest had she tried to live in her previous style in Brighton, but in Athairton it was ample. They decided to sell the Lagonda and buy a car that used less patrol, plus a bicycle for shorter trips.

Mr. Nialls promised to take her surplus fruit, eggs and vegetables in return for groceries and David planned to get her some pigs. Lugh had found a swarm of bees and was going to set up a hive for her and Marcus suggested keeping a carp pond instead of goldfish. His offer was rejected but promises of fishing expeditions with Arthur and Lugh compensated for any loss of face over his suggestion. Patiently, the Athairtons fed them hope and happiness until faith transcended time's momentary grief.

The July sun beat down on to the earth and the soft rain seeped through the soil, feeding Sam's vegetable kingdom. Isabelle spent her days digging and picking until her hands were stained to the colour of the earth and her face was burnt like a bronze apple. Her baskets were filled with bright young carrots, fat shiny courgettes, champion cucumbers and giant marrows. Peas and young turnips were frozen quickly, as were the red- and blackcurrants that hung inside their cages like large clusters of grapes.

Raspberries and strawberries were abundant as were the cherries. They hung in big black bunches, like Christmas decorations, while the bells that Old Sam had tied to the branches tinkled in the breeze and frightened away the birds. The pigs snortled through the orchards with squeals of pleasure accompanying every juicy find.

Lugh had helped Marcus to build their sheds and the boy would stand proudly watching them as if he were a father overseeing his children's progress. He had also had the chance of helping some of the farmers with their sheepshearing, and his sense of achievement could be seen in his newly acquired farmer's gait.

The broody hens presented Isabelle with three sets of chicks, so other pens had to be built to protect them from the other jealous chickens. There was never any wasted food in the Nodens kitchen. Unlike in the cities, every scrap or leftover was placed into buckets for the pigs or chickens. Paper, cardboard, tins and bottles were all collected by the villagers and sold for recycling. The money collected was all spent on the village school.

When Lugh arrived with the bees Marcus and Isabelle watched him warily from a distance. He had placed the hive by her herb garden, close to the thyme, and rubbed the inside with balm because, as he told them, the bees loved the smell and would always return to it.

With netting draped over his head, his hands covered by thick gloves, and his whole body zipped into a boiler suit he resembled an alien spaceman as he carried the seething bundle towards the hive.

Mac yapped with excitement around his feet, miraculously avoiding being stung. "Those beasties can still get inside all that," Old Karen said as they stood watching Lugh depositing the bees inside the hive.

"You'll get good honey from that swarm, mind," she added, "and if I get stung, it'll only be Dis Pater thinking about my arthritis."

Mac disgraced himself a few days later. Marcus let out an angry yell when he caught the sneaky Cairn cocking his leg over the young ash.

Old Sam came to the rescue by placing stakes around the tree while Mac, tail drooping with shame, watched from behind the summer house.

"While we're here," Sam said solemnly, "we'll see to those old moles, we don't want them digging up this 'un." They were all given a rota for stamping.

"Like this," Sam shouted, dancing and stamping his feet all over the surrounding ground. "They've got sensitive ears, those old moles. You bang on their roof and they hate it." He then planted caper spurge all round the tree. "That'll fix them buggers," he said triumphantly.

Marcus' friend Nicky phoned to tell him that his family were driving through Exmoor on their way to their new home in Devon. He asked whether he would like to be picked up and come and stay with them for a week. Although he was thrilled at the chance of seeing his friend, Marcus didn't want to miss Lugh's birthday on the first of August.

Lugh however assured him that he wouldn't be offended by his absence and that they could all have a second celebration when he returned. That all agreed, Isabelle invited Nicky's parents to stay for lunch.

It was pleasant to get out of her old clothes and dress for visitors. Weeks had passed since she had worn any make-up. As she welcomed them she felt quite cool and serene and thought how different it had been in the past when she had shaken with fright the moment she'd been introduced to strangers.

Jim and Diana Evans were friendly people with smiling, open faces. They greeted her with warm handshakes and offered their quiet condolences.

After showing them around and listening to their approval for her ideas on self-sufficiency, they retired indoors for lunch where the Evans explained to her their fears for the future and described their land, which was near Sheepstor, south-west of Dartmoor.

Like many business men Evans was in despair over Britain.

"You know, I feel as if apathy has pushed our country back into a state of feudalism. Only the rents and leases are now in the hands of banks and large conglomerates. My business was in

London. By the time I'd conformed to restrictive legislation, paid higher rates and taxes, I could see that I was being forced into the position of a vassal. That's why I'm opting out and putting everything into this place in Devon. I suppose I'm anticipating the 'peasants' revolt'. And I want my family out of the way when it happens."

It was like listening to echoes from Chris, she thought, as she sympathised with him.

Diana was as anxious as Isabelle had been about her move. She had always lived in a town and was finding it hard to readjust to their new, quieter way of life. She gratefully accepted all Isabelle's advice and promised to keep in touch with her.

"I shall probably be on the phone to you all the time," she said. "At least I don't feel so isolated now."

Marcus was exuberant. The Evans had horses and loved hunting and they promised that he would return home with at least a rabbit. It was agreed that they would bring him home on August the fifth. Nicky could then stay with the Carringtons for a week. He wanted to go with Marcus on the salmon-fishing trip organised by Arthur and Lugh.

Just before they left for Sheepstor Marcus drew her aside and showed her his present that he'd made for Lugh. They stood along his window ledge, looking like large pieces of ebony and ivory. "I bought this kit Mum. See, they're plastic moulds. The chess pieces are only plastic but they look super don't they? Do you think Lugh will like them?"

Isabelle assured him that Lugh would be thrilled, especially as he had made them himself.

They drove off after tea, leaving Isabelle to her familiar solitude. The sun was still overhead as she walked through the gardens towards the summer house. A cloud of tortoise-shell butterflies, hovering over the lobelia, dispersed as she passed, clustering together again after the sounds of her rustling skirts had died away. As she breathed in the splendour of the view her blood tingled with excitement. She felt at one with the screaming merlin as it swooped across the sky towards the moors.

Pulling off her shoes she fondled the warm grass with her toes. The soft rhythm from the distant tractor echoed in syncopation with the gentle grunting of the pigs. The harmonious buzzing from the bees joined with the melodious wail of the chickens and forced her pulse into a sympathetic beat with nature's orchestra. Her feet joined the primitive sound, sensually dancing their own enchanted movement.

Deep from within her soul her eternal sound reached towards the ether and returned to surround her in a spiritual temple containing celestial hymns to the glory of life. Wildly she danced, weightless and free, her arms reaching like roots to the spiritual nourishment. Endlessly she spun and turned until the grass grew damp in the growing shadows. The sun, a red, passionate giant, rested on the sea. She sank to the ground, wet with perspiration and happily exhausted.

She could sense him.

Turning her head quickly, the first glance revealed a stag sitting on the gate. Blinking her eyes cleared the illusion and she saw instead Lugh. An apple branch across her line of vision had given the appearance of antlers.

She sank back on the grass laughingly helplessly. He stood against the sun, looking down at her. "I thought you were a stag," she laughed.

Slowly he unbuttoned his cardigan, watching her. "You found the temple," he said smiling at her.

She sat bolt upright.

"How did you know?" she asked. "I could hear your music." He started to laugh at her bewilderment. "I've had my temples too. Those moments are when Dagda sings to you and you are learning to listen."

He wrapped his cardigan around her shoulders and kissed her gently on the head. "But," he said lifting her to her feet, "after dancing like that you'd better keep warm." The warm musk smell from his cardigan crept round her.

"If you'd like to risk your stomach, I've prepared dinner at the cottage. Do you think that's a good idea?" As he took her arm and gently walked her back to the house, a hot smouldering ember, at the base of her spine, burst into flame. While they walked down the lane towards the village wisps of midges lay suspended in the air. They ran through each swarm, brushing the tiny insects from their arms. In front of open doors and windows, folk gathered outside their cottages in the main street, talking together in the last moments of the day.

They called out to Lugh, as he and Isabelle reached his gate.

"Are you making the supper tonight, Lugh?"

"I am," he replied.

Cackles of glee came in response. "Don't forget to stir with the hair of a doe," an old farmer called out. "Isabelle, mind he don't stir it with his paint brush," shouted Old Karen.

The sky had turned a deep purple. Veins of magenta clung lovingly to the sky as the sun's skull tipped the horizon. Venus announced the approaching, hesitant night.

He had laid the small table carefully and placed a posy of carnations in the centre. She sat sipping her wine and savouring the delicious aromas creeping into the small lounge while he talked to her from the kitchen. He spoke cheerfully about the art dealer who was going to visit him the following day. Twelve of his paintings were being taken to London to be hung in the Mall Galleries. She was thrilled for him and asked whether he'd ever had a showing before.

"Oh yes," he replied as he served the soup, "I sell quite a few." It was fresh mushroom soup. She praised his talents as a chef.

"Ah, but wait," he said mysteriously. "This is something that you have never eaten before." He served the next dish and watched her reactions carefully. It was in a spicy sauce and tasted like pork. Her taste buds probed the unfamiliar food, searching for an answer. "It's pork of some sort?"

"No." He grinned. "I'll tell you what it is over coffee but I assure you that you've never had it before." Isabelle racked her brains during the raspberries and cream, but she couldn't think what the meat could have been. While he made the coffee she sat, well-fed and content, waiting for the answer.

"It was hedgehog," he declared triumphantly, "I told you that you'd never had it before."

"Hedgehog?" she gasped. He roared with laughter at the expression on her face.

He recounted the comical stalking of the hedgehog until her sides ached.

A deep yearning forced its way through her body and reflected in her eyes. He saw the emotional tidal wave and held it in recognition until it created a seething, bubbling cauldron of passionate longing. Breaking the gaze, he sighed and looked down at his hands, clasping them and frowning with concentration.

"Do you only sell your paintings in London?" she asked politely, sounding like the Queen Mum. "No," he replied, "all over the country."

"I used to love going to the art gallery in Brighton," she said, reflecting over her past private moments.

"Did you ever look at the artists's name?" he asked.

"No," she replied thoughtfully. "Now you come to speak of it, no, I don't. I just look at the picture."

"I thought so."

"Why?" she asked.

"Because you have one of my paintings, hanging in your bedroom."

She caught her breath.

"Cow and Cow Parsley," she whispered.

"In the whole gallery, that was the one and only picture that meant anything to me."

"So it should have done," he replied seriously. "It was looking for you."

They sat in silence for a long time.

Isabelle's heart was pounding.

Suddenly he stood up. "It's late, I think it's time that I took you home."

They walked back to Nodens, hand in hand. Fire rushed through her body with every change of pressure from his palm.

Outside her door, he took her face into his hands and looked searchingly into her eyes.

"I'll see you on Wednesday."

He kissed her quickly and walked briskly away.

CHAPTER ELEVEN

It was a beautifully moulded silver hand. She had found it in a small antique shop, tucked away in a small side alley that led from the main shopping street in Minehead. Endless polishing had restored the blackened piece to one of gleaming, silky beauty that is only possessed by old silver.

She thought that it would be a symbol of their friendship, like the Dürer hands that she'd always admired.

She planned to present Marcus' chess pieces and her present at his party. His birthday card had been dropped through his letter box first thing that morning. Bridget told her over coffee the previous day that as the celebration was also to commemorate Llugnased that it would be appropriate for her to wear white.

Not only was it the tradition, but as it was the first time that she had taken part in a Celtic ceremony spiritually it would be the right colour for her. Luckily, she had a white silk shirtwaister, stored away in the attic. A dress that she'd worn when she'd been in her twenties. Washed and pressed with the hem taken up a little it was perfect for the occasion.

All the people were bringing contributions to the feast. Isabelle prepared a large bowl of creamed chicken salad and another large bowl of trifle, decorated with the raspberries from Nodens' bushes.

From the first moments of waking that morning she had been dominated by a glorious sense of anticipation. Across the moors a slight haze foretold a perfect summer day. Sounds of distant hammering reminded her of the booths that were being put up for the fair.

Today, not only was it Lugh's birthday but her introduction to the group ceremony. All the endless hours of study in order to absorb Bridget's teachings on chant and sound were going to be put into practice. Lugh had told her that they had all experienced the 'Temple of Music' that she had discovered when dancing by the summer house.

"No-one can tell you how to discover these truths," he had told her. "We can teach you all that we know, but truths are only revealed to you when you are ready and only Dagda knows when that is; but we all rejoice with you when you find them." She wanted that union that they all talked about and knew it would be revealed to her during the ceremony.

By half past eleven it was a scorching hot day. The festival was starting at noon with horse-racing for the men. So after delivering her contributions to Bridget they set off together for the large field, about a mile away from the village, where the fun was to take place.

Ribbons and streamers fluttered in the warm, southerly breeze. Brightly decorated stalls offered prizes for games of chance. There were pitches for throwing the horseshoe, tossing the old wellington boot, throwing sickles at a stand of corn and felling the wooden post.

All stood silently waiting for the horse-race to begin. A dozen horses stamped impatiently at the end of the field. Old Sam hovered near them, clutching his starter's flag. A tent, set up by the stalls, seethed with activity as the villagers placed their fivepenny bets on the horse of their choice.

Lugh's mount, a white stallion, pawed at the air, anxious to be let free, to charge with the other horses across the field through the woods and back again to the waiting crowd. The riders were stripped to the waist. Their brown bodies gleamed in the blazing sunshine. They were riding bare-back, relying on their balance and their grip on the horses' manes. Their bare feet soothed the animals' flanks as they waited for the signal.

Sam brought down his flag and they were off.

A babble of conversastion broke out amongst the crowd, each villager speculating upon the chances of his chosen bet. They craned their necks to catch sight of the first rider to emerge from the woods on to the distant hills.

A streak of white announced Lugh as he hurtled out of the woods and galloped up the first hill. The distance between the white stallion and the other horses grew wider as Lugh rode him across the hills. The stallion disappeared into a gully and then suddenly raced across the field again towards Old Sam's waiting flag.

The crowd yelled and cheered as each sweating rider and horse galloped back up to the starting point. Then the winners rushed to claim their money at the tent.

Immediately, the stall holders started vying with each other for the people's attention. Arthur's voice boomed out as he stood, his red face beaming, by the horseshoe pitch.

Isabelle threw the horseshoe three times but never managed to catch the iron. Bridget chucked the rubber boot and narrowly missed Dermot's ear. Pies were bought from the pie stall. Their golden crusted shapes were marked as "Granya's Apple" or "Olwyn's Cheese Tasty", "Gwynneth's Cornish Pasty" or "Isabelle's Blackcurrant". All the people's talents were on show from Maeve's knitting to Lugh's paintings, sales of which were to raise money for the village.

She sat on the grass with Bridget, contentedly sipping Karen's home-made lemonade and eating a pasty while they waited for the tree chopping. The children's pony races were in progress while the best-trained dog competition took place in another part of the field. A small boy called a large sheepdog by whistling, as his father had taught him.

Isabelle looked down at Mac, who was gazing longingly at the well-trained sheepdog, and kept her foot firmly on his lead. She knew what the wicked old Cairn would do if he was given half a chance.

Arthur, Dermot and Brian, a sheep farmer, were standing by their respective poles. Sam blew the whistle. At once the crowd shouted for their favourites as the men raised their axes and commenced to chop the wood.

Their muscles rippled and their sinews stood out as, panting with exertion, they raced to fell their poles. Lugh wandered over to Bridget and Isabelle.

"Happy birthday!" they chorused. Bridget hugged him.

A small knot curled in Isabelle's stomach. Then he turned and hugged her and her stomach uncurled and dropped, somewhere in the region of her knees.

There was a yell of triumph from Arthur as his post tipped and crashed to the ground. She was released from Lugh's hot hug as he rushed over to grab Arthur and declare him the winner.

Beckoning waves from the women on the pie stall reminded them that it was their turn to serve.

She and Bridget wandered over arm in arm, with Mac panting behind.

Once there, the dog stretched out in the shade of the counter, close to the cooling chests for the ale.

Sticky hands handed them small coins in return for the pies.

Isabelle looked into the friendly faces asking for "one of Karen's" or "two Bridget Pasties, please Isabelle," and she was aware of how quickly they'd accepted her as one of them. In Athairton, people were addressed by their Christian names. To hold reverence for an individual's skills and talents was natural but as each felt his own importance and worth as a member of the community no deference to another was ever either expected or given.

The crowds drifted towards a clearing where the wrestling was to take place. Two sturdy lads from neighbouring farms were competing for the prize of a silver cup. Isabelle and Bridget watched all the people mingling around the ring. Some stood in small groups. Others watched the wrestlers. Children teased each other then scattered into different directions, swooping back like swallows, to start the game all over again.

Old men remembered their youth as they jerked their arms sympathetically with each splendid action of the struggling opponents. Lugh and Arthur stood together, yelling and shouting for their favourite, occasionally pushing each other and laughing like overgrown children.

Isabelle felt caught up in their exuberance. Bridget watched her intently as she laughed at their antics. Feeling the penetrating gaze at her side Isabelle pulled her eyes away from Lugh, flushing with embarrassment.

"You love him, don't you."

"Well," Isabelle blushed, "I'm far too old to think of him in that way."

"Rubbish," Bridget replied. "You know that's rubbish as well as I do. Anyway, I asked you whether you loved him?"

Isabelle remained silent.

A roar from the crowd drew her attention back to Lugh who was dancing with joy at his favourite's victory. Her eyes filled at the sight of his open, innocent rejoicing. "Yes," she whispered, "I love him."

Bridget clasped her tightly. "I knew you did," she said, "I just wanted you to admit it to yourself; you must know how he feels about you."

"But I'm so much older," Isabelle sniffed. "That's not true," Bridget laughed. "Your soul's got a long way to go before it catches up with Lugh's." She looked at Isabelle sternly. "Twelve years? Do you think that a man like Lugh cares about such superficial problems? He loves you for yourself, you silly woman." She wiped Isabelle's tears with a tea towel. "It's the soul he's interested in," she said quietly.

As if sensing their conversation Lugh and Arthur wandered over to them. "I think I'll try one of your pasties, Bridget," boomed Arthur, his face flushed dark red from the sun. "And some ale to match your face?" Bridget joked.

"I'll be like a beacon tonight with this face," he laughed. "I can stand on the pathway and light the way to the picnic."

Lugh's hand touched her arm lightly. "I'll try an Isabelle's Blackcurrant, I think." Her face blazed until it almost rivalled Arthur's. It was as if the statement made to Bridget earlier was written in fiery letters across her head. She bent down to the trays under the counter in order to give herself a moment's composure.

"There's one up here," he said, watching her curious behaviour.

"Ah," she exclaimed, aware of the trickle of perspiration running down her forehead. He grinned at her. "You've got very hot, serving in the stall."

"Well, you can come in and help her," Bridget said quickly, coming to her defence.

Arthur hurried off with Bridget in the direction of the tent, which had been cleared of all the betting slips and now had a queue of young girls outside, waiting to have their fortunes told.

Isabelle felt as if she was inside a sauna. His very presence increased her body temperature to that of near boiling point. "Here, sit on this crate," he said, moving one of the boxes on to its side. Gratefully, she sank on the seat.

Fetching some ice, he wrapped it in a tea towel and placed it firmly on the back of her neck. "Thank you," she gasped, clutching it desperately in order to rid herself of the growing heat.

"And when it's cooled you down you'd better give it back to me. I'm burning up."

The fair was all over by six o'clock. After the last sickle had been thrown at the stand of corn a group of women then plaited it into the rough shape of a woman, then hoised it high above their heads, to signal the end of the fair.

Women wandered off in small groups while the men all set about dismantling the tents and stalls.

Isabelle walked slowly back home, with Mac sagging heavily on the lead. Hot, sticky and confused, she made her way to the bedroom, peeling off her clothes and dropping them on to the floor. The air was quite still, with no suggestion of a breeze. She lay on the bed, letting her skin luxuriate in the coolness of the linen coverlet.

The three ravens dipped their beaks into the soft lawn, searching for moisture. Isabelle stood watching them from the bedroom window.

The silk clung to her shoulders. despite the momentary relief from bathing, her body heat returned. Her skin embraced the coolness of the dress.

She ran across the lawns to check the pigs. Her bare legs were burnt to coffee colour from the day's hot sunshine. The pigs lay still on the grass, grunting gently, their pink skins waiting for a night breeze. Gentle squawks came from the chicken run as she checked the water. The chickens stared at her with eyes like glazed alcoholics.

Mac's hairy form was stretched out along the stone scullery floor. Gently, she stepped over him and collected the presents from the kitchen table.

Her heart fluttering with excitement. she drove towards

Culbone. The rays from the sinking, orange sun were still hot. They lit the winding trail of villagers making their way towards Bridget's farm.

She parked on the moor, near all the other cars and made her way down the dusty track towards White House Farm. "Grab yourself a piece of wood," one of the women advised her, gathering some twigs from the hedge. "Everyone has to throw a bit on to the bonfire." Hastily she looked for some, taking care not to dirty the white dress. The unlit bonfire stood in the centre of the cow field.

They all walked towards it, threw on their wood and then turned to make their way towards the terrace where Bridget and Lugh stood waiting to greet them. Isabelle placed her stick on the bonfire and then followed the others. The women's light pastel-coloured dresses bobbed up and down as everyone stepped up the hill towards the terrace. In the evening light it gave the illusion of a host of moving flowers.

Isabelle was the only one dressed in white. She was surprised. Obviously she had misunderstood Bridget when she had told her that it was a tradition to wear it. Unless it was only for newcomers . . . .

Bridget was dressed in a glowing yellow kaftan. In the distance she resembled a stately sunflower. Next to her, Lugh, in cream trousers and a loose white smock, greeted the guests as they arrived.

They greeted her warmly and she handed her presents to Lugh. Slowly, he unwrapped Marcus' gift.

The others gathered round as he undid her present.

He withdrew the silver hand and held it in the sunlight for them all to see.

There were gasps from the villagers.

"Nuada's hand," shouted Karen.

Isabelle was puzzled. There were cheers and stamping of feet. Lugh drew her to him and kissed her on the lips. The growing throng shouted their approval.

He looked at her solemnly. "Thank you, Isabelle, it's the most beautiful present I could have been given tonight."

He put his arm around her and drew her close to him.

"Stay beside me," he whispered.

"It's the blessing of Dagda," Old Sam was yelling. The late arrivals were all informed by those that had been present of Isabelle's gift to Lugh.

They seethed with excitement until they sounded like a swarm of bees. "What does it all mean, Lugh? What have I done?" she asked him. He took her arm, wrapped it round his waist, then holding her closely to his side walked with her towards the bonfire.

"The history you will learn," he said, "but, days ago, after the battle of Mag Tured, which was a battle over the powers of darkness, Lugh, or Lug as some people say, was the victor. Nuada of the silver hand was dead and the Tuatha De Danaan made Lugh their king."

The sinking sun smiled its last red ray of light and then vanished into the sea. They stood in darkness, alone by the bonfire.

She felt the warmth of his breath as he whispered to her. "You were guided by the universal spirit, Dagda, to present me with a sign."

He smoothed her hair gently. "These people know one meaning of the sign, that's why they're so happy."

He released her and bent down to set light to the bonfire, striking a match against a petrol-sodden torch. He threw the torch on to the mound of wood and a huge flame shot into the sky.

The watching villagers raced towards them.

"But," he said, holding her tightly to his side again, "I know a more serious meaning of the sign and I can't share that with you yet."

The Athairtons had all linked arms and were moving slowly around the fire, chanting in whispers. Isabelle watched the people as they circled around them and from deep within her Brigantia remembered the ceremony stretching back through the centuries. Turning to Lugh, she smiled her recognition.

"Lleu babir," she whispered.

He saw the spirit in her eyes and loved her. Only Erinna was yet to come and then they would be complete.

Bridget served the hot soup on the terrace. Groups of people sat around balancing their simple wooden plates and drinking soup from wooden bowls. Loaves were passed among them to break roughly and pass on. A trestle held all the communal food which they would eat after the symbolic drinking of the soup. The corn dolly, plaited at the end of the fair, stood in a dominant position over the sumptuous spread.

Music and dancing helped the digestion as, mellow and happy, the people sang and laughed through the evening. Just before twelve, Bridget collected all those who were to take part in the mystical ceremony and led them into the quiet atmosphere of the house. Candles were lit and the symbolic articles placed as they had been before when they had congregated at Nodens.

They sat quietly in the circle, their eyes focused into the centre. Isabelle felt relaxed. She had practised the disciplines with Bridget. Now she would see for herself.

A tiny pinprick of light appeared, flickering just above the ground.

Bridget started the sound which they all echoed. Slowly, the light grew, spinning like a top and beaming its rays on to each one of them as it spun round. Bridget changed the sound and they all followed suit.

The light grew so bright that it almost hurt her eyes to look, but she did as Bridget had instructed her, kept concentrating, and didn't panic. Just when she thought she could bear it no longer, Bridget started the chant and they all joined in, keeping it controlled and steady.

The light stopped still and lifted its position to a place high above them.

Bridget asked who was wanted in the circle.

The light moved to Isabelle and hovered over her. "Get up and go into the centre," Bridget instructed her quietly. Isabelle did as she was told and waited anxiously.

The light hovered over her and then moved slowly over to Lugh. "Enter the circle," Bridget said firmly.

The light followed him and circled over their heads.

It began to descend, circling around Lugh and Isabelle in a clockwise movement, forcing them together as it circled around their shoulders and slowly worked its way down around their feet. Lugh reached for her right hand with his left and placed his right hand on her stomach.

She looked to him for guidance and he indicated to her silently that she should place her left hand over his right hand. Next, he leant towards her and placed his forehead against hers. A bolt of what seemed like lightning passed through them causing a shudder that gripped them together. Isabelle felt as if she were floating through a thunder storm. Everything before her eyes turned a deep shade of blue.

In the floating blackness of time, Erinna heard a call. Stirring herself against the eternal sea she willed herself to Lugh, fighting to find the endless tunnel that would lead her to him. Far beyond was a circling light. She pushed herself towards it, aware of Brigantia's guiding signal.

The dark blue faded and the natural colour of the candlelit room returned. Isabelle looked at Lugh who was focusing his eyes to the real light.

"Come back to your chairs," Bridget whispered quietly. She had tears in her eyes.

Isabelle returned to her place and sat down. A wonderful sense of peace filled her entire body. Her arms felt as light as air. Her head felt as if it was supported by wings.

More chanting followed, but the light had gone. Then it was all over and Sam was kissing them and saying, "Bless your love." Bridget folded them to her and kissed them and the others joined in, clustering round them and hugging them, then touching them with a sort of reverence.

Brigantia looked at Lugh and understood. They smiled at Sam who was staring at them with wonder.

"Ba nassa damsa indingen ut uair chein," Lugh said softly to him.

With her head resting on his shoulder, Lugh drove her home.

The full moon followed them through the winding Exmoor hills.

The call kept changing direction. Erinna struggled to move towards it, until at last she was pulled into the spiralling tunnel. Feverishly, she fought her way towards the light.

They walked together through the orchard and towards the

summer house. His arms wound around her and lifted her towards him. He was more forceful than she could remember him being before. His male smell filled her nostrils as he held her to him. His slight stubble scratched her chin. She felt a sudden panic as the memory of her first day at Nodens filled her consciousness.

The unseen arms had held her like this. The smell that had been in the air around her and the roughness that had brushed against her chin had been Lugh. He saw the panic in Isabelle's eyes and held her more gently. He kissed her softly on the head.

Was she going mad? She could have sworn that it was her father kissing her goodnight.

He pressed his body closer to hers and kissed her on the mouth. The velvet lips drew her into a world of ecstasy. Brigantia smothered Isabelle's fear and hungrily offered bold response, primitively answering his demanding mouth.

The moon sent its warm vibrations down to the great Nodens oak. A soft breeze regulated the pulsing heat from their bodies as they stood naked by the tree, their skin luminous in the moonlight.

Through the ethers Erinna drifted until she felt the moment draw closer.

Brigantia rested, conserving her strength to help Erinna.

Isabelle stood apprehensively, vulnerable in her nakedness.

A thousand butterflies winged around her body as his soft mouth drew her to him. Gentle hands stroked her breasts so that she drifted into an ocean of sensations.

Erinna was poised, waiting for the moment of descent.

The warm earth welcomed her soft back and the sweet smell of grass filled her senses. He crouched like a smooth, marble lion, over her, his muscles reflecting on his gleaming arms. She felt the light hair of his smooth hard stomach as it brushed over her soft yielding belly.

She gasped as he thrust, the exquisite pain searing through her body. Her ears were filled with the rhythm of a thousand heartbeats.

Remorselessly he probed, demanding from her complete union.

Erinna was pulled like a shooting star from the heavens. Joyfully she fused with Brigantia and showed herself through Isabelle's eyes.

He saw her and recognised her.

Tears filled his eyes as he whispered. "I'll love you for eternity."

Her sound echoed through the hills as Erinna and Brigantia, as one, united with Lugh and created the eternal strength and love of the whole woman.

The insignificant Isabelle, the shadow of imposed systems and false standards, died. In her place, the wisdom of eternal female, the wise woman, devoted, loving, and with the strength of a lion's mate, rose like a phoenix, with a cry of surrender.

CHAPTER TWELVE

She stirred. The light from the warm morning sunshine coaxed her into wakefulness. Turning away, she caught sight of his dark hair on the pillow. She stared at his wonderful, sleeping innocence, until sensing her gaze he opened his eyes.

Smiling sleepily, he reached out his arm and drew her to him. Burrowing her face into his warm neck, she breathed in the perfume of closeness and wriggled with the pleasure of their completeness. She searched his waking body for reassurance and was immediately swept into a passionate response.

As she prepared breakfast, her body ached, reminding her of each moment of their lovemaking. Like a fallow field turned by the plough, life throbbed through her entire being.

They talked intimately. Each declaration strengthened their trust in each other. Any fears that Isabelle might have had about her age, body, or any other physical embarrassment were soothed away by his great understanding. He compared her stretchmarks to a beach touched by the tides of creation. His need for her soul, as Bridget had told her, was of first importance.

"I gave you my gloves for protecting your hands. They were a present to me from my foster mother and I treasured them, but I loved you more. I painted for you all my desire and love. You saw the walls but your soul understood. I have been part of you always. My soul followed wherever you went. I waited for you to join me."

For three days, they spent every moment together.

They walked and saw as one, the colours made more intense by their united love.

The villagers, seeing them walking together, smiled their approval and shared the reflection from their glowing harmony. They laughed together, reducing each other to tears with their shared humour.

They devoured each other in the act of love, discovering endless exquisite pleasures until together they entered the Temple of Music and joined the Gods, in celestial union. Words were no longer needed. Each one was bound in the same awareness. Apart, they were as one, able to attend to their respective chores, yet spiritually never separate.

The collective conscious of the Tuatha De Danaan had joined them in marriage. No one, except in peril of his life, would dare attempt to come between them.

It was agreed that he would often stay at his cottage. Not only to concentrate on his art but as one of the leaders of the village he needed time to think about the welfare of the Athairtons. She, too, needed time on her own. Apart from her everyday chores and the affairs of Nodens she had her important studies with Bridget.

Now, she understood the urgency of the situation. As "sister" to Bridget, she carried responsibilities that were far greater than she had originally understood. She was now Brigantia and Erinna combined. Within her was the power to effect change and alter circumstances. As the second daughter of Dagda she had pluralised the strength that was needed to form the 'Brigit', the female defender of the Tuatha De Danaan. The men were meeting at the next full moon to aid the nearly formed 'Brigit' in prophesy. Then there would be a meeting of all the elders in the village to discuss the implications of the prophesy and the future plans for Athairton.

Marcus arrived back on the fifth.

His young face grinned with pride as he presented Isabelle with his hunter's bounty. Three hares and six rabbits. The Evanses stayed for lunch and related their hunting stories with relish. Apparently they had all had a wonderful time. They had all experienced the joys of village life in Devon and also taken part in festivities on August the first. The fair that they described to her seemed to have been similar to the one in Athairton. Nicky had won a prize for a pony race and Marcus had won one for archery. Marcus, blushing slightly, told her about the dance held in the village hall later that day. Nicky added the fact that two girls had taken a shine to him. Yells and guffaws followed as the boys, laughing hysterically, told them how the two girls had followed them around for days, nearly getting themselves shot, as rabbits, in their attempt to flirt with them.

The Evanses set off at teatime, leaving Nicky behind to stay for a week. While the boys were occupied Isabelle asked the Evanses, before they left, about the possibility of buying a horse for Marcus. Jim Evans told her that there was a young stallion that the boy had ridden every day until it was almost a part of him. A deal was made with promises for the delivery of the horse to be made on his birthday during the half term.

While Nicky was unpacking Isabelle spoke to Marcus about her feelings for Lugh, treading warily in case he thought she was being disloyal to Chris. He listened quietly while she told him that they were in love and how much he meant to her. "You will get married then?" he asked.

She knew that for his sake she would have to comply with convention. She sensed Lugh's consent. "Yes."

"I suppose you'll sleep with him then?" he asked her, looking out of the window.

"Yes," she replied.

He turned back, looking worriedly at her. "You won't go and die in childbirth or anything silly like that, will you? I mean, you're not that young, are you? Or are you like Daphne and can't have any more?" His expression was that of concern, not disapproval as she had feared. His loss of one parent and fear of losing another has given his face a pinched, grey look. She hugged him closely.

"I'm not going to die, I have too much to do. Anyway, Lugh would do nothing that would place me in danger. You do approve of him, don't you?" she asked. "Oh yes," he sighed, relieved that his worries were unfounded. "Lugh's super and I suppose . . ." he paused and searched his emotions. "I'll have a best friend kind of father now." He was so lanky that it was difficult to hold him on her knee. Awkwardly she managed, holding him as she had when he had been a tiny boy, giving him the warmth and security that he still needed.

While Isabelle picked some runner beans and the first of the cauliflowers the boys skinned the rabbits with great dexterity. Soon the tantalising smells of rabbit stew filled the kitchen. She had made a plum tart for pudding and a light fluffy chocolate sponge. She covered the cake with a mound of chocolate whipped cream and stuck a candle in the centre. By celebrating the birthday that Marcus had missed she hoped that they could overcome any difficulties when trying to form their new relationship.

Lugh arrived at seven-thirty, carrying the chess pieces that Marcus had made for him. With open arms he welcomed the boy, who was so unused to men demonstrating their feelings that he blushed furiously. Isabelle joined them and the three clasped each other, oblivious of young Nicky's presence. The male contingent retired to the lounge to swap hunting stories while Isabelle returned to the kitchen to supervise the supper.

It was a noisy mealtime, the boys boasting about the hare that got away and then singing some rude renderings of 'Happy Birthday'. A tough chess competition started between Marcus and Lugh after supper, while Nicky tactfully withdrew to the kitchen to discuss with Isabelle the best way of helping his friend through the predicament.

When he realised that his good friend Lugh had not changed in any way towards him but that he had the bonus of a closer relationship Marcus was filled with happiness. Plans were made to hunt salmon. Lugh had seen a whopper which they all promised would be placed on her table. Sleepily, the boys made their way upstairs. The noisy bathroom sounds echoed as she clung to Lugh, her restraint forgotten as he smothered her face in kisses. Gently he placed her in the chair and discussed Marcus' feelings.

He would arrange a marriage in the church, he told her, in three weeks time, so that Marcus could feel part of the whole arrangement. In the meantime, he would stay at the cottage and join them occasionally for meals. "I want him to know that I'm not taking his mother away from him but joining you both as a family," he said, "and even after the ceremony we'll restrain ourselves in front of him. He must never be made to feel in the way or embarrassed."

She listened as he spoke, aware of his compassion and love for her most precious son. How right Bridget had been when she had spoken of his old soul and the wisdom that he carried with him. No wonder the villagers loved him. No petty thought occured to him. He was as man was supposed to be, gentle in his strengths and certain in his truth.

After Lugh had left for the cottage she crept into Marcus' bedroom. She smoothed his hair. His eyes flickered as she kissed his head. "I'm glad about Lugh, Mum," he murmured.

Clutching the picnic basket and fishing tackle, Lugh and the boys waved goodbye. "Get the fish kettle ready, Mum," were Marcus' last exuberant shouts as they set off on the trail of the giant salmon. The recipes for the use of herbs were endless. From the use of the runner bean leaf for the simple boil to the use of elder flower blossom tea for colds. She had filled in so many exercise books of Bridget's potions that they filled an entire bookshelf in Nodens' lounge. Bridget explained to her that there was always an antidote for every illness, supplied by nature.

The simple nettle could stop bleeding. Its boiled leaves also created a tea that could relieve fever. Dandelion leaves could be used to test pregnancy. The foxglove could help the heart. She showed her how to hunt for sphagnum moss, the herb that acted as an antiseptic. She was learning too about how to cast spells. Simple ones on her own, stronger healing ones when she worked with their combined strength.

Bridget was getting more excited as their united strength grew more powerful. For so long she had been the only one. Detached from her 'sisters' she had been like a head with no eyes. Now with one 'sister' helping, her seeing eye had returned. At the next full moon she would use the combined strength to look for the other 'sister', Belisima.

As she helped to mix the different formulae Isabelle started to laugh. Bridget looked up to share the joke. "I can't help thinking," said Isabelle, "that if we went on the open market we could rival Boots."

She returned to Nodens by three o'clock in time to ask Sam to dig up some of the new beetroot. He stood leaning on his garden fork, examining one of the onions. "It's a thin skin they've got this year," he said. "There'll be a lot of those nasty colds around October." "Why, Sam?" she asked, always ready to listen to the old man's pearls of wisdom.

"'Onion skin, very thin,
Mild winter coming in.
Onion skin thick and tough
Coming winter cold and rough'," he chanted. "Well, you can see thisun's thin. Mild winters always confuse, you see. The birds get so they don't quite know when to go. The animals mope and the humans, well, they don't put on enough clothes and when they do they're too hot and get colds.".

She cut some parsley. It grew quickly, a tribute to her newly found strength. She was careful to avoid the bees' flight path as she picked more herbs from the garden while offering a silent wish for the success of the salmon hunters. They arrived back, soaked from a sudden cloud burst, but triumphantly carrying the biggest salmon that Isabelle had ever seen.

Only half would fit into the fish kettle. So, after endless photographs had been taken to verify their future fishermen's tales, the prince of fish was cut in half. She stayed in the background, content to allow their male companionship to continue through the evening. She accepted their praises for her cooking with the serenity of an earth mother.

The following three weeks passed quickly. Marcus delighted in the long summer days, spending the time exploring the moors with Lugh. Nicky's parents collected him and plans were made to share the collections from school. Isabelle, volunteering to take them back for the Autumn term on the eleventh of September, agreed to stay overnight with them on the tenth. The Reverend Morrigan put up the banns for the wedding which was planned for the twenty-ninth of August.

David and June were asked to come and they accepted cautiously. David had immediately pointed out to her that she should turn the ownership of the house to Marcus so that there could be no legal complications in the event of her death. "I'm sorry, Isabelle, to be so morbid, but I've got to think of what

Chris would have advised in the event of your marriage." He said apologetically, "I'm sure Lugh is a nice chap but I've got to think of your interests."

Lugh was sympathetic when she told him. "I don't want David worried about Marcus' position. Of course you must do all the right legal things for him." He grinned at her. "But you're not going to die for a long time."

The Athairtons would not come to the ceremony.

As far as they were concerned she and Lugh were already married. However, Karen and Old Sam told them that they would come. Not only to keep Lugh company but because they wanted to see old Morrigan clear the churchyard of all the confetti that they were going to throw. "It'll be the hardest work he's done in years," cackled old Karen.

She felt that as she was an old friend she ought to ask Daphne. Besides, she had promised her that she would ask her down to Nodens for a holiday. "You're what?" she shrieked into the phone, when she told her. "I don't believe it," she gasped. "That lovely young man. You crafty cow, I'm livid with jealousy." She and Emma arrived two days before the ceremony, bringing a length of blue ribbon, which they insisted should be tied round "Somewhere or other, love. A bit of borrowed from Brighton." Lugh left them well alone for the first day of the visit as if sensing the bawdy air that Daphne brought with her.

"Are there any more Lughs left in the village?" she giggled. "If so, I've brought my butterfly net. Where do you find them?" They talked long into the night with Daphne probing for information about her sex life, which was firmly kept from her. Daphne sighed with frustration.

"The watch-seller was my last bang and it wasn't even a bang, just a damp squib. I tell you Isabelle, if I want a man I think I'll have to move into the country too. They're all queer in Brighton or looking for a rich widow, not a subsidised divorcee. I tell you the number of rich cows in Brighton is disgusting. They spoil it for us all. I mean, who can compete with old bags that buy them cars and silk shirts."

As if embarrassed about having any romantic or finer feelings, she thrust a package at Isabelle and left the room. Inside was a beautiful copy of Desiderata, mounted on a board. She looked at it with appreciation knowing that Daphne in her way wished her happiness, but because of her enforced role as sophisticated woman of the world she would never be able to communicate in words what she felt.

After the ceremony David and Lugh approached each other but after only a brief conversation all David's suspicions and feelings of discomfort disappeared. Isabelle watched them smiling and talking and felt a great sense of relief. She had hoped that her only close family would accept Lugh for the man that he was and not hold any prejudiced opinions about him. As Karen had promised, they were showered with confetti. She and Sam became so hilarious that they sat on a grave stone yelling and swinging their legs blasphemously. It was like everyone's wedding nightmare of the arrival of terrible relations. Marcus and Emma were so used to the well-behaved etiquette of other church occasions that at the sight of them they wept tears of uncontrollable mirth. David and June joined in and they all rolled out of the churchyard like scrumpy soaked vagabonds.

Karen had insisted on making the cake in the shape of a horseshoe. Surrounding the cake was a bower of flowers. Every room in the house was filled with the scents from the summer bouquets. Lugh caught her eye and smiled. The Athairtons had played their part in the day's ceremonies by creeping into the house while they had been in church and conveying in flower language their feelings. There were bunches of red and white chrysanthemums, symbolising love and truth, clematis for mental beauty, little bowls of dandelion represented love's oracles and wild honeysuckle for devoted love. The bower was entwined with ivy for friendship and fidelity in marriage and dotted with lily for purity and sweetness. In every corner were red and white roses for unity.

"But how wonderful," exclaimed Daphne, turning to Isabelle and Lugh. "They must think so much of you both," she added wistfully.

They all ate heartily, relaxed in each other's company, then after Marcus had practically squeezed them to death with his hugs they escaped to Lugh's cottage.

They clung together as the sun in eclipse with the moon.

Their abstinence, having controlled the tides of their passion, was banished into a second of time as they breathed into each other's souls their continued eternal love.

Daphne stayed on for a while. She delighted in helping with any gardening or feeding the chickens and pigs. She even seemed content to help in the arduous task of freezing the fruit and vegetables. Marcus adapted quickly to Lugh living with them and after his teenage curiosity had been satisfied and he realised that his mother's personality had been in no way altered by her wedding night he entered into the new family relationship gladly. Now he had an ally in the female-dominated Nodens and all the warmth and companionship that Chris had never given him. He would often escape to Lugh's cottage. Occasionally, if Lugh's work was finished, Arthur would probably be there and they could luxuriate in a profound male discussion. One evening, much to Isabelle's surprise, Daphne burst into tears.

They had been sitting talking gaily by the lily pond in the enclosed garden when there had been a lull in the conversation. Isabelle had enjoyed the silence of the evening and watched while the fish popped up for the stray hovering insect. "I'm so shallow," Daphne wailed.

Isabelle put her arms around her. "What's made you suddenly say a thing like that?" she asked. "Oh, sitting here, being here," she sobbed. "I'm not jealous, no that's a lie, I am jealous. I want this too. What went wrong for me, Isabelle? Sometimes, you know, I feel like a drag queen, not a woman any more."

Isabelle thought of her friend and the differences in their lives. She, who had once clung to Daphne, desperate for friendship when she'd been lonely in Brighton, was now needed by her. "In what way do you feel shallow?" she asked. "Oh, I think it's since I've been here. Pottering around the garden, like I used to do as a child, talking to Sam and Lugh and feeling inadequate because," she sniffed, "without my party, witty conversation, I've got nothing to say to people."

"I know how you feel," Isabelle sympathised. "But I couldn't even offer wit, when I first moved down here. Do you know what was the most marvellous thing for me?"

"What?" Daphne wiped her eyes and looked up at her. "Laughing spontaneously," she smiled, "and really feeling happy at the same time, not forcing a smile so that my ears ached to keep it on my face." A throaty chuckle rumbled out of Daphne. "Oh, I know what you mean, I need a pound of night cream sometimes after some of the people I've been with."

"Well here," Isabelle continued, "I'm free to be myself. Happy or sad as the mood takes me and no one makes me feel guilty about the truth of my feelings."

"I try so hard," Daphne said wistfully. "I watch my appearance, read all the things to see what's going on, but I still feel lost. Why?" Isabelle thought of all the spiritually dead faces that she had seen on her last trip to London. The expressionless women, the only light in their eyes that reflected from neon strip lighting as they walked desperately around the glossy stores, buying unnecessary make-up as an excuse to achieve a free offer. An aimless meandering that bound them in dependence on substitute joy.

Anger grew, as Brigantia challenged the suppression of British women and demanded their freedom. Freedom from the zombie women who, masquerading as humans, fed the soft vulnerable women the philosophy that the achievement of orgasms was paramount to love. Freedom from the glossy pedlars who offered escapism while buying their souls, dangling baubles of fashion to lead them away from themselves and offering a diet of delusion against any nourishment of truth.

"Have the courage to be yourself and you won't feel lost anymore," she said, hugging Daphne to her. "And stop putting yourself down, or I'll thump yer." The next day, Daphne appeared downstairs without a scrap of make-up. She announced her new self defiantly. "Right you lot, here I am, take me as you find me." The effect on them all was hilarious. Gales of laughter rocked the breakfast table, with Daphne laughing louder than any of them. Lugh got up and kissed her. "Welcome Daphne," he said. "I'm glad you let me meet you."

Bridget called over to meet Daphne and spent some time wandering round the garden talking to her. She had hoped that this could have possibly been the third 'sister'. She knew that she would come to Nodens and suspected that Belisima's soul might be locked in another sad human being like Brigantia's had been. She sought the signs, playing the game with Daphne and asking her to choose one of the three articles that she carried with her. Lugh assured her that Daphne was not the one and after an afternoon of subtle testing she had to admit that he was right.

Daphne loved Bridget. Talking to Isabelle about her later she remarked on her wisdom. "To think that I once thought she was a witch," she said. "Although, I suppose she is a sort of white witch, if you think about it. You know, teaching you all those things that I've seen in your bookshelves." Isabelle smiled but didn't reply. Her teachings were sacred and she made a mental note never to leave the books in an exposed place again. Luckily, Daphne had only stumbled upon the recipes for herbs, but spells, in the wrong hands, could be dangerous.

Laden with fruit, eggs and vegetables, Daphne and Emma waved their farewells, leaving behind the tightly grouped threesome. Daphne thought as she drove away that there was a serenity in the group that seemed to send out waves of peace. Lugh, Brigantia and MacOc watched the departing guests, seeing two fragile souls returning to a land of conflict, armed only with momentary hope.

CHAPTER THIRTEEN

David called on them, bringing enough straw and chicken feed to see them through the winter. In return, Lugh and Marcus loaded on to the truck all the fruit and vegetables that weren't grown at Carrington Farm. He stayed for lunch, and after complimenting Marcus on the size of the jugged hare that they had just eaten, moaned about the farm taking up so much of his time that he'd had no chance to take part in shooting. Promises were made that as soon as Marcus and Lugh had time to go hunting again some grouse would be delivered to his door. Lugh had to spend another two days finishing a painting for an exhibition and then he and Marcus were going to spend a whole day chasing game.

Marcus reminded David of their conversation during the Easter holidays, when he had told him his plans to study farming and asked him whether he could come and help on the farm for a few days. David hung his head in shame. "Marcus, I'm sorry, I clean forgot what with all the things that have happend." He looked at Isabelle. "Shall I take him back with me now?"

"Do you want to go today, Marcus?" She'd hardly got the words out of her mouth when the boy was thundering up the stairs to pack a holdall. Her maternal concern was apparent as she issued instructions and warnings. Lugh calmed her. "Let him go, Isabelle. He's a sensible young man."

She felt niggly and agitated. Outside the rain teemed down and she felt cold and cross.

She had wanted more time on her own with Marcus. First he had gone with the Evanses, then he had been with Lugh and Nicky. Daphne and Emma's arrival had taken more of her time and now he'd gone off with David. Tears rolled down her cheeks. All the wonderful serenity that she had felt during the last few weeks vanished, leaving her in a confused vacuum. Her back ached, so she decided to take a bath. She lay in the bubbles, sulking like an angry child. As she dried herself she cursed the jugged hare that now made her feel sick.

Lugh arrived home to find her sitting in the darkened lounge gazing miserably out of the window. Without saying a word he prepared a fire and put the kettle on for tea. Soon she was sitting in front of a blazing fire, munching a biscuit and sipping the strong sweet brew.

He stroked her face and kissed her. A niggly worm ran through her body. His insistent fingers sought her vulnerability and demanded a change of mood.

Her body fought a battle with him, resisting his gentle requests. Firmly he lifted her onto the floor and after removing the protection of her dressing gown moved against her, his body's warmth demanding submission. He captured her mouth and re-awakened the ashes of her passion. His flame surged through her, kindling her body back to life.

Remorselessly, he plunged deep within her, driving away the barrier that had appeared. Her moaning and cries of protest only helped to increase the urgency of his forceful thrusting until her pain became a convulsion of exquisite yearning, bringing an animal strength and returning passion to his insistent challenge. Bathed in sweat, his back scratched by her desire, he filled her pleading body with his burning life force, holding her face tenderly as she sobbed with relief. Exhausted, they slept until the dying embers in the fire allowed the chill night air to surround their entwined bodies, sending them, murmuring in soft voices of love, to their marital bed.

She apologised the next day. "I can't think why I was like that, Lugh," she said. "I think I just didn't feel well or something."

"I enjoyed the battle," he said smiling. "Anyway, it's over. You're allowed to have bad moods, you know. Wait till I have one and you can do the same for me."

The night of the full moon had arrived.

In the afternoon she went to Bridget and confided her fears that she might let her down when it came to the ceremony. Bridget smiled. "Every one of us has felt that before our first prophecy, slightly scared and worried about losing our strength.

All you must do is remember the tree and its colours."

Isabelle paced the room, blotting everything from her mind except the tree of life and the numbers on the diagram that she had painstakingly drawn. She chanted the names of the sacred numbers and remembered the twenty-two letters and the colours.

Lugh had stayed at the cottage the previous night, meditating and consulting with the elders. She would not see him until after the ceremony. The future of the Athairtons was too important for them to be distracted for a moment from their spirits' true purpose.

She had also been careful about her diet, eating only fruit and drinking only water while she waited with Bridget for the men to arrive. They filed into the room and sat waiting silently, until the time was right. Then in accord they rose and formed a circle around Bridget and Isabelle.

It was Isabelle's role to assist, using every ounce of her strength and concentration. She breathed in deeply, assisting Bridget as she went through the banishing ritual of the pentagram, stabbing the centre as she faced the four positions, north, south, east and west. A glow appeared in the centre of each pentagram. Their bare feet and the hems of the kaftans had been dipped in water. Dagda and the other Celtic Gods were summoned to protect them in their vulnerable state within the circle. The cauldron stood on the altar. Bridget took her hand and tapped the cauldron with it . . . several times.

A surge of energy shot through Isabelle as she joined in the chant. It was not Brigantia. She knew the spirit that dominated her thinking. This was another force and it took Bridget by surprise. Her seeing eye was suddenly extended. The vision overwhelmed her in intensity. She swayed. She now had the strength of three 'sisters' instead of the expected two. She could feel Brigantia helping her but was the other spirit Belisima or a marauder? "Identify yourself," she demanded.

A faint whisper echoed through Brigantia's and Bridget's souls.

"It is I, Belisima."

"Where are you?" they both asked silently.

"I am somewhere near to you," the small voice replied.

The Prophecy began to appear to Bridget.

The 'sisters' held their energy together.

Before the seeing eye loomed the heavens, normally viewed from the field at Whitehouse Farm. The sun was opposing Saturn, Jupiter, Mars and Mercury. Libra dominated the western world. The stars turned to snow which crowded across her vision. Slowly the snow turned to churning foam in the sea, out of which came large fish propelled by fire. They flew like birds into the bright, clear blue sky. Then the whole sky turned to flames. A hundred suns beamed their scorching heat towards the fields. Then there was utter darkness.

Tears rolled down Bridget's face as she felt the death of Dagda and heard the thunder of his dying wail.

There appeared out of the blackness a gloomy grey world out of which stared MacOc, the ruler of the underworld.

The faces of the Athairtons, their faces lit by flickering candlelight, appeared, surrounded by darkness. A mist grew in the seeing eye which cleared to reveal the fatherly face of Dagda.

His voice reverberated through their bodies.

"MacOc will bring the answer."

The men retired to Lugh's cottage to discuss the prophecy while Bridget and Isabelle, exhausted after their ordeal, sat drinking cups of tea. "Belisima is here, in Athairton," Bridget said quietly. "She's obviously trapped, as you were, in a confused body."

"It must be one of the women in the village," replied Isabelle. "But who?" They fell asleep, waiting for Lugh, who didn't return until the morning. He arrived, ashen-faced and sank down onto one of the kitchen chairs, burying his face into the warmth of Isabelle's stomach. Silently Bridget made some coffee while Isabelle nursed his head in her arms. They ate breakfast quietly, the women waiting to hear his interpretation of the prophecy. "What time is Marcus coming home?" he asked Isabelle.

"About ten o'clock I think," she said, puzzled that he was not more forthcoming. "I'll see to the chickens and the pigs," he said, getting up and putting on his boots. "When Marcus comes back, he'll complete the interpretation."

Deep in thought the women carried on with the morning

chores. The post office van arrived with a buff-coloured envelope for Marcus. Isabelle placed it in her pocket and went to join Bridget. They sat by the kitchen door, welcoming the sunshine, their tired faces turned like flowers towards the sun's hot eye. "Do you understand the prophecy, Bridget?" she asked the older woman.

"Yes," she replied. "But anything to do with the future of the Athairtons has to be interpreted by the men. In that way, the true will of revelations cannot be influenced by our conscious will.

"This was your first attempt. Although Brigantia knows as much as I do, each lifetime, we must start again from the beginning, humbly, and when we have complete integrity, then we progress into this lifetime's learning. You are not yet free of the conscious will. This you must learn. When you are, then it will be nearly time for you to lead the 'Briget' and you will then have to find me and teach me all over again. So are we reborn, through humility, to learn greater knowledge."

Isabelle remembered her recent petulance with Lugh and understood what Bridget was telling her. Concentrated thought was so powerful that if for a moment it was influenced by emotional instability, it could be dangerous. This was the reason why those who sought power by perverting the use of magic usually ended up sick or insane. The wise women, like Bridget, knew that true knowledge was only found through self-knowledge, humility and service.

Isabelle understood that her emotions were not yet ready for anything other than assisting and this the older woman had told her in the kindest possible way. David arrived with Marcus. Lugh appeared and welcomed them, then offered David a coffee. He refused the offer sadly. "I'd love to stay, but I've got a thousand things to be getting on with," he replied. "Isabelle, you've got a natural farmer there in that boy," he said, ruffling Marcus' hair fondly. "June sends her love and as soon as we get a bit more time, when the kids go back to school, you and Lugh must come over for supper." "We'd love to," she answered. "Here's a letter for you, Marcus," she added, suddenly remembering the buff envelope.

The boy opened it apprehensively. "I think it's the O level results." His eyes scanned the list. Then he let out a yell. "I've got the lot. Grade 'A' in Science." Isabelle hugged him while the others offered their congratulations. His face was red with pleasure. "I think I'll get a Coke." He leapt in the air and rushed inside the house, shouting his farewells to David as he ran. David laughed. "I think he was getting a bit homesick, actually. He had a terrible nightmare last night, gave us all quite a fright."

"What time was that?" Lugh asked quickly.

"Oh, about ten past twelve. Frightened June out of her wits." He clambered into his car and started the engine. "I'll see you soon, bye for now." They watched the wagon disappear out of the gates, then Lugh went straight inside the house, followed by the two women.

Marcus was grinning from ear to ear.

Lugh asked him about his nightmare. The boy's mood changed. "Oh, Mum, it was really creepy. I was yelling at you all . . ." "Who do you mean, all?" asked Lugh. "The whole village," the boy went on. "I was trying to get them into an old silver mine."

"Where was the mine?"

"I think it was about where Dermot's place is, near the sheep farm."

"Yes," Lugh urged him on. "How old were you, Marcus? Think carefully."

"I was a man, because I had a beard, and it was summer," he replied. He rubbed his hands across his brow. "We had candles and then there was an earthquake or something and the people were all screaming."

Isabelle sensed that he was getting upset and looked anxiously at Lugh, trying to halt his questions. "And after the earthquake sound," Lugh asked him gently, "were you all right?"

"Yes, but the animals were hard to control, I think that was all." He looked at Lugh. "Why?"

"David told us you'd had a nightmare." Lugh got up and put the kettle on to the Aga.

"I'm going to phone Nicky, Mum, and see if he's had his results." Marcus disappeared from the room.

Lugh looked towards Bridget. "How long will it take you to

work it out astrologically?"

"I can probably find it by tea time." She rose from the kitchen chair and gathered up her things. "Is there a silver mine near here?" Isabelle asked.

"Yes," he replied. "It hasn't been worked for about two hundred years and it's covered by bushes."

"Where is it?"

"Exactly where Marcus said it was," he said seriously. "Behind Dermot's place."

Lugh took Bridget back to the farm. He was about to see Arthur and the other men in the village about arranging an emergency meeting for that evening. "Could I come too?" Isabelle asked. "No," he replied firmly. "I'll come home for lunch, but I can't tell you yet until I've spoken to the others."

She spent the rest of the morning baking and preparing lunch, with Marcus sharing with her all his secrets and his hopes. Smells of sweet pastry and roasting chicken mingled together filling the kitchen with a peaceful atmosphere of homeliness. As she scrubbed out the roasting tin and laid it out to dry on top of the Aga Marcus touched her gently on the head. "It's funny Mum, sometimes you're like a Mum, like you are now, and sometimes I feel as if you're my sister, do you know what I mean?" She nodded. "I know exactly what you mean."

Brigantia looked at MacOc in recognition. They had to learn the humility that Bridget had spoken about before their true strength could be revealed. Until then, each one would have to discover slowly, learning with momentary flashes of understanding what their true purpose in the world was to be.

Lugh arrived back for lunch. His face was still drawn and worried-looking. He held them both in his arms and in a husky voice told them that he loved them very much.

After lunch he disappeared again, informing her that Sam wouldn't be working that afternoon and that he would be late returning. They spent the afternoon picking fruit and working in the garden. Blackberries sat fat and juicy in the hedges just waiting to be picked. The tomatoes swelled red in the greenhouse. Marcus suggested that they should try growing their own vine so that they could have their own grapes. They laughed at the thought of the three of them pressing the grapes for wine with their feet.

After yet more freezing and bottling they settled down to tuck box lists and then watched a terribly predictable American film on television. Cops chased crooks with inferiority complexes. "If America's the sort of place that they show on television then I think it must be pretty scary, don't you?" She agreed.

"And do you know what I find really frightening?" he said.

"What?" she asked, watching a woman exuding sincerity as she asked the public to solve their problems of inneficiency by stuffing a chocolate bar into their mouths.

"That one man could be responsible for wiping out the human race," he said, gazing at the flickering screen.

She treated his pubescent spots with calomine lotion and delivered yet another lecture on the value of washing before he retired to bed. She curled up on the sofa and waited for Lugh to return. Mac, grateful for any moment without competition, stretched lovingly across her lap. He arrived back just after midnight looking tired and gaunt. Hastily she made him some supper and then afterwards massaged the tension out of his shoulders. "What did Bridget find?" she asked. "It's just after May the twenty-first, in four years' time," he whispered. "So we have to work fast."

Her heart thudded as he told her what she had suspected all along. "We've been down to the mine," he went on, "and if we work every day in shifts, we can have it ready in time."

They lay together, his head resting on her breast, looking through the bedroom window at the star-filled heavens. "This is Eden," he said quietly. "This beautiful world. Why do they have to look for answers when the truth is staring them in the face? Our knowledge is so beautiful yet when the evil ones find it they use it to banish us yet again from our holy temple of music."

"Will we survive?" she asked, tears running down her face, as she thought of everyone that she had ever encountered in her life. The surly railway porters, even the bad-tempered shop assistants glaring with resentment at every shopper, became monuments of beauty when she considered their obliteration. "Yes," he answered. "We have to fulfil our purpose."

The grouse and pheasants hung from the larder shelves, their swollen heads staring at the ground. Rabbits dangled too, reminders of the successful day's hunting. Isabelle carefully selected one of each and placed them in a bag, thinking how much Daphne would appreciate a share of the hunt. A selection of fruit and vegetables and some eggs completed the surprise gift for her friend. She set off with Marcus for the Evan's house. It lay about a mile and a half from Meavy on the Tavistock and Ivybridge road. Compared with the soft feminine lines of Somerset, Dartmoor was hard and masculine, with its granite rocks and heath-covered hills.

Mournful notes from the rare gold plover gave an added atmosphere of loneliness as they stopped to look at a ragged heap of granite called the Tor. They passed through a collection of cottages and an old stone church before arriving at the large Evans' estate. Horses grazed or sheltered under the large trees. They turned their heads curiously when the car drove up to the stern granite house. Bloodhounds sounded the alarm and immediately the Evanses appeared to greet them.

Marcus disappeared with Nicky to see the horses as soon as they arrived, leaving Isabelle to relax in the cool lounge with a very welcome cup of tea. Diana warbled cheerfully about how romantic it was that she had married again, then a tour of the house followed, with the Evanses confiding in her all their plans for the rooms and the land. "I hope this won't shock you," Jim said shyly, as he indicated some stairs to the cellar. "Shock me?" she enquired. At the bottom of the stairs was a large steel door. He opened it and walked inside. She gasped.

The door was about twelve inches thick and led into a concrete cellar which was the size of a small room. A small vent in one wall was the only interruption in the white enclosed space. "Just in case," he said sheepishly.

Lugh had told her not to mention anything about the mine to anyone so she couldn't share the secret with the Evanses. She did, however, express her relief that they had provided a shelter for themselves, adding that she and Lugh also wanted to make preparations for any eventual emergency.

She enjoyed their warm hospitality and appreciated the

obvious care that Diana had taken, preparing the boeuf stroganoff and the delicious blackberry fluff for their supper. During coffee, Jim felt compelled to justify the existence of the shelter. "I was on a business trip to Switzerland last year," he said. "The Swiss really are a nation of survivors you know. They've been shrewd enough to stay neutral through two world wars and now they're making sure they'll survive a third. Nearly all of them are building shelters — the mountains are full of caves." Diana pursed her lips in studied disapproval. Jim ignored the silent reproach. "There never seems to be a week without a battle or a revolution starting somewhere. I just wonder how long it's going to be before we're all sucked into one of them. And then there's the terrorists. One of those groups is quite capable of sparking off exactly the sort of thing I'm talking about."

He paused and Diana changed the subject to herb gardens. They talked about her plans for improving the whole kitchen garden area. All terrifying thoughts were succesfully excluded from their conversation.

They set off early next morning with the car filled with squash racquets, tuck boxes and school trunks. The two boys appeared in their school uniforms that transformed their usual cheeky appearance to that of very sober-minded young men. It was a long tiring journey, broken by a break for lunch and a pause for ice-cream and another for stretching their legs. They arrived by six o'clock and joined the other cars unloading chattering boys who were ready to start the autumn term. The partings were always painful for her, so her usual tears accompanied her to Daphne's house.

She was exhausted when she reached there. The conversation with the housemaster, explaining her re-marriage, and the tears after leaving Marcus, had combined with the effects of the long journey and given her a splitting headache. After hugging Daphne and giving her the presents from Nodens, she retired to bed, apologising weakly for her worn-out state. She awoke in the morning feeling violently sick. As she heaved in the bathroom, she made a resolution to find out about the train services in the future. Marcus, after all, was sixteen and quite able to travel on his own. She felt so weak that she decided to stay for another night and phoned Lugh to tell him not to worry.

"If you feel no better in the morning, stay there and I'll come and get you," he said, his voice registering concern. She spent a pleasant day with Daphne, gossiping about the odd acquaintance in Brighton and reliving past-shared times together. She was still feeling tired from the journey so again she retired early to bed and felt dreadful pangs of homesickness as well as a yearning for Lugh. Although she still felt squeamish the next day she started off for Somerset, the thought of another day away from Lugh being more than she could bear.

He was waiting for her as she drove through the gates.

She clung to him, absorbing his strength gratefully, as he held her in his tender embrace. He tucked her into bed and drew the curtain. Outside, she could hear the sounds of the chickens, clucking in the evening sunshine. The distant whine from the tractors sounded like humming bees. She was home and safe with Lugh and drifting into a peaceful sleep.

She stumbled out of bed in the morning, startling him with her violent movements. Nausea overpowered her until she retched gratefully in the bathroom.

He was watching her as she crept back into bed. He smoothed her brow. "Are you all right, now?" he asked, kissing her damp eyelids.

"I'm fine," she replied, sighing deeply. "Oh, I haven't been that sick for years."

She breathed in deeply and opened her eyes.

He was smiling. Gently he ran his palm over her stomach and pressed her womb. It was as hard as rock. Slowly he unbuttoned her nightdress and inspected her nipples. They were turning into a soft brown. He laughed, "No, I don't think you've been like this for about seventeen years." He gathered her into his arms and held her tightly.

Red blisters had formed on the big coarse dandelion leaves. Bridget stood with Isabelle and looked at them. "Well," she announced triumphantly. "Now we know where Belisima has been hiding, don't we?" Bridget and Brigantia laughed with joy and the young unseen 'sister' smiled in the sea of tranquility.

CHAPTER FOURTEEN

It was ridiculous. She had thought that she'd gone through the change of life and that pregnancy was impossible. Apart from a few weeks of retching and the urge to sleep a lot she felt as strong as an ox.

The gardens were ablaze with colour. Dark red apples hung in the orchards, fuchsias bobbed gently, dahlias and chrysanthemums stood proudly, their different colours smudging into a blurred rainbow as the air around them shimmered with heat. She felt as placid as a contented cow as she padded around the house, seeing to the chores and enjoying each remaining summer day in the garden. The last stooks of corn were brought in from the fields and placed on their sides in sheltered corners of the different farms. They would be kept there until the following year when they would be ploughed back into the earth. In the meantime the grateful birds ate the seeds, darting around the stooks excitedly.

She joined the other women and learnt how to make corn dollies from the remaining straw. Their conversation and giggles resembled the gentle clucking of the farmyard chickens. When every single farm had collected its harvest the Athairtons held a supper, with the men relaxing with cider, knowing that all their work had been done. A large plaited loaf dominated the table. Rounded cheeses from Bridget's farm added bright spots of yellow to the groaning trestle that offered the tasty talents supplied by the women. They waited until the men who were working down the mine returned and then the pudding was brought in. Old Karen carried it in, helped by the older women. The sight of it was greeted by cheers from the waiting villagers. Then there was a reverent silence as Bridget cut into it, revealing an assortment of delicious meats and releasing the most tantalising smells.

A dance followed, the music getting quicker as the evening progressed and the food was shaken down. "That's enough dancing for you." Bridget said firmly as Isabelle was about to embark on a wild Gay Gordons. "We don't want to shake the life out of poor Belisima, do we?"

October crept in. The summer weather lingered on. Only the colder evenings warned the Athairtons to hurry with their preparations for winter. Fruit was gathered and stored, bottled or frozen. Crab apples were gathered and jellies made.

Mac followed Isabelle everywhere as if sensing the need for her to be protected. He satisfied his guarding instincts by chasing the squirrels as they searched the trees for the newly-formed nuts.

Her lessons with Bridget continued. Her meditation she found much easier in her new relaxed condition. It was during these quiet months that occasionally Belisima would whisper to her. Brigantia would listen to her 'sister' as if she were an unseen voice on the end of a telephone. All that an observer would see was Isabelle sitting in the walled garden, silently watching the changing colour of the leaves.

Samhain was approaching. The beginning of the Celtic new year. On the night of October the thirty-first all the elders would again meet at Bridget's house and at midnight all the barriers between the living and the dead would be removed. The ceremony was perhaps the most important one of the whole year.

Isabelle worked hard at her studies in astrology, urged on by Bridget. Her psychic powers were developing rapidly as Brigantia grew stronger. She was now able to see the aura around a plant or person and detect whether they were healthy or not. At night, she would lie in bed smiling, as she watched Marcus asleep in school or her spirit wandered into the mine to watch Lugh on his night shift. Once she had returned to watch herself, lying in bed, but felt a little frightened so returned into her body immediately.

On the twenty-fourth, the sky was filled with birds, grouping and regrouping into a moving, swirling cloud of winged specks. Isabelle and Lugh watched them as they suddenly took a decision and swept across the sky towards warmer lands, disappearing into the distance like a black magic carpet. Coils of black heavy clouds arrived the following day to release heavy rain, forcing the bright orange and red leaves to flutter damply to the ground. The nights brought frost and a warning of winter. Robins claimed their territory for their survival, looking hungrily at the berries in the garden's winter larder.

Marcus arrived back for half term with the Evanses. They clambered out of their car, creased with weariness from the journey. They gratefully agreed to stay the night before setting off for Dartmoor. Over a dinner of grouse the boys related their gossip from school and the usual horrendous stories of arduous army corps manoeuvres. They ended their patter act with a hilarious demonstration of marching while attempting to salute Jim who stood in solemnly as army captain, his past national service making him the only one in the house qualified in army matters. Lugh joined in, trying to achieve the salute with some sort of dignity and failing dismally, much to the boys' glee.

They talked long into the night, Jim expressing his fears about the rising political extremism.

A memory of Chris flashed through Isabelle's thoughts as she listened to him talking . . . Chris as he had been that night when she had listened to him telling her that they were going to move from Brighton. "They're polarising," he had said.

Isabelle could see it in Jim. He was normally so gentle; now he was heated with aggression as he spoke of England being ungovernable. She watched Lugh's face and his expression of compassion for the man's deep fears.

Brigantia echoed the understanding, knowing that none of the people of whom Jim spoke were the causes of the country's troubles, but like a Middle Eastern riot before an earthquake the people were sensing the next movement of the world's destiny. Jim went on to explain to Lugh about his shelter and how he was storing food.

"The Mormons do it you know, Lugh, it's part of their religion to be prepared for catastrophes, and the Swiss, those ever-surviving gnomes, have shelters built into every new home." He suddenly broke into hysterical laughter. "Imagine a world populated only by bankers!"

While Jim continued his theories on world problems, Isabelle confided in Diana about her pregnancy. Diana insisted that in future the boys travel by train as even she had found the journey tiring. Plans were made for Marcus' stallion to be delivered to Arthur's barn, where it could remain hidden until his birthday.

Lugh's hands were roughened by the work he was doing down the mine. Gently, she rubbed cream into them as he lay back in the bed gazing at her sleepily. "I'll tell Marcus tomorrow," she said, "when I'm on my own with him, don't you think?" He nodded. "MacOc will gain his strength by Samhain, then he will understand and not be frightened any more."

"I thought it might happen," Marcus said thoughtfully. "I talked it over with our biology master. He said you'd probably be all right if there's no history of strangeness in the family."

"Strangeness?"

"I mean extra genes or hereditary illness or something."

"No," she laughed, "there's nothing strange about me, I don't think, and there's none of the inherited illnesses that you're talking about in the family, and I've had German measles and also a thorough check up by an excellent gynaecologist in Taunton, so I should be all right, Marcus. Don't worry." They watched Mac weaving in and out of the bushes during their walk towards Athairton. The weather, as Sam had predicted, had turned mild again. Having reassured himself that his mother was in safe hands Marcus turned his attention to the activities in the old silver mine, asking innumerable questions until Isabelle became desperate about her lack of knowledge. "Ask Lugh," she found herself saying, over and over again, until she eventually lost his attention. He strode purposefully towards Athairton where his questions would be answered.

He left her when they reached Nialls Stores and headed for O'Leary's place. It was as if the very knowledge that time was limited gave the Athairtons the appreciation of each day. The different weather was talked about. People lingered, reluctant to miss one moment's happening in the busy village.

Stories were exchanged inside Nialls Stores, as the women shopped slowly. Unlike the frantic neon-lit stores in the cities the little shop was full of shaded corners where Isabelle would browse, joining in with whatever conversation appealed to her while she searched for any exciting looking jars that could be added to her larder. "When's Marcus' birthday, Isabelle, is it soon?" Olwyn asked her. "The twenty-eighth," she replied.

"On Punkie night!" Maeve squeaked. "Oh, that's lovely! We'll have a party already for him. There's going to be fireworks and a fancy dress party. We'll all be there," she said. "Only with all the men working down the mine we didn't know whether to have it this year, but the kids would have gone mad. So we grabbed some of the younger men and put them in charge of the fireworks and we'll use records for the dancing. Do you think he'd like to come?"

"I'm sure he would," Isabelle answered. "But I'll ask him and let you know, shall I?"

"Lead is what you need."

She heard Marcus' agitated voice raised high in discussion with Arthur as Gwynneth led her through the small hall and into the lounge. Marcus was on the floor in front of the fire, pouring over plans of the mine. Arthur sat beaming in his large easy chair, smoking a pipe and listening to the boy's enthusiastic suggestions.

"Morning Isabelle," he said, tapping his pipe gently. "We'll be having him down the mine as soon as you give the word."

"Can I go Mum?"

She fought her usual over-protective maternalism and agreed, then rememberd to ask him whether he would like to attend the Punkie celebrations. "Punk? Oh, Mum, I hate all that row, they're weird anyhow, I've told you before that's not my scene."

The others burst out laughing.

"Not Punk, Marcus. Punkie!" Arthur said. "It's a sort of firework tonight, I suppose, a kind of Hallowe'en, you might say, nothing to do with those funny fellows on television with funny coloured hair."

"Oh," Marcus smiled sheepishly. "Sorry. Well, you never know, and you must admit it's a pretty funny name, punkie. What is a

Punkie anyway?"

"It's a cut-out swede that looks like a little lantern," said Gwynneth. "It's in the shape of a face. You put a candle inside. That's a Punkie. I'll show you how to make one." She disappeared into the kitchen.

"You'll enjoy the evening, lad. There'll be all the young people there, dancing, shouting and making a noisy nuisance of themselves," said Arthur. Gwynneth returned with a large swede and an evil, sharp-looking knife. She proceeded to show them the art of Punkie making, deftly scooping out the centre, then cutting the shape of a grinning face into the skin. Arthur struck a match and held it inside.

"There you are, one Punkie."

Isabelle wandered up to Lugh's cottage on her own, Marcus having run over to Maeve's place to tell her that he would be coming to the celebrations. He was deeply engrossed with his painting and didn't hear her come into the studio. Music aided his inspiration. Mozart fed his own creativity. She watched him quietly, enjoying his momentary unawareness of her presence.

He turned round quickly. "How long have you been here?" he asked, looking slightly dazed. She nuzzled into his arms. "Only a little while, you looked so peaceful." She looked at the painting. It was a scene depicting 'Athairton in Autumn'.

The little figures of the villagers, all wrapped in scarves and coats, seemed alive as they poised on the canvas, about to go about their daily business. "It's beautiful, Lugh."

Over lunch, Lugh and Marcus made plans to go to the mine that night. While she listened to their conversation she found herself reflecting on the changes that had brought her to this moment of time. She felt she had changed, like the seasons, and was now waiting expectantly for the next metamorphosis. She watched Lugh and Marcus as if from a great distance, observing their animated discussion and going through the motions of smiling and nodding to them, but her mind floated sifting through the memory, the events that had happened during her time in Nodens. Each month, it seemed, had drawn her further away from the person that she had been when she first arrived. Compared with how she was now, it could have been an entirely different woman walking through the stone gates and looking apprehensively at her future home.

Mac lay on his back in front of the fire, his paws held limply in the air. His rounded old stomach sagged towards the ground and he snored contentedly.

She felt a strange sadness as she looked into the crackling fire.

Her reflective mood had continued through the evening. Lugh had taken Marcus down to the mine, so she had meandered about the house, almost reliving the moment of departure from Brighton.

The love-child in her womb would be born on May the first, if her calculations were correct. How long would this little life have to enjoy the countryside, the discoveries of nature's wonders, before the sentence of darkness, and what kind of strange or unfriendly world would be waiting for her emergence? Isabelle and Erinna felt the sadness of mothers-to-be all over the world and shared their fears for the future. Brigantia would not play host to the weaker feminine emotions inspired by Erinna. Maternalism was fine and good but she represented survival and a sense of purpose.

Order would come after chaos.

Any negativism could destroy the foundation of faith and hope in the Athairtons. What use was clinging love, no matter how ecstatic, if it took away the strength to grow and adapt to new challenges. Belisima whispered quietly to Brigantia.

"Don't let her weaken me."

On the day of Marcus' birthday Lugh collected the horse from Arthur's place early in the morning and tethered it to the gate by the kitchen garden. He then joined Isabelle for breakfast and they both waited for Marcus to appear. His hair was standing on end as he stumbled into the kitchen and was greeted by "Happy Birthday".

"I'm afraid your present's outside," said Lugh casually. "It was too lumpy to bring into the kitchen."

"Where outside?" he asked. "Oh, it's by the kitchen garden, I think," Lugh replied. Marcus dashed into the garden, ignoring Isabelle's wails about catching a cold. He reappeared after several yells and shouts, his face alight with joy.

Apart from lunchtime and dusk, they didn't see Marcus all day. He and Ayatollah, as he had christened the horse, explored the surrounding hills and fields together and arrived back exhausted.

Eerie faces peered from the street corners as children held their Punkies in the dark night air. Then in accord they started to chant as they made their way towards the village hall and the field beyond.

"It's Punkie night tonight!
It's Punkie night tonight!
Give us a candle, give us a light,
Or we will give you a terrible fright!"

"Boos" and "Yaahs" followed the end of the verse when the children lifting their lanterns for the most frightening effect, tried to scare the watching adults who, feigning abject terror, put some money into their rattling collection tins.

Squeaks of glee came from the tiny toddlers who believed in their frightening powers and the occasional wail from one whose candle had blown out. The procession finished up in a field where the youths, Marcus among them, threw torches on to a huge bonfire which was the signal for the firework display. Rockets soared to the sky. Isabelle clutched herself, feeling as excited as the children as red followed by blue and green screamed into the sky. Bangers frightened them, catherine wheels entranced them. Dogs barked in protest and they all applauded the silver and gold rain.

Then came the expensive one, the finale to the evening's display. Gasps greeted the explosion that lit up the sky. Fireworks were released from a central cluster that formed its own nucleus of orbiting fire. The whole sky was turned into day as the light grew in intensity. The sighs of wonder turned to awed silence. Isabelle saw Bridget. Her face, lit by the fiery light, registered the anguish of premonition.

After the smaller children had paraded around the hall, the king and queen Punkie were chosen. Then one by one they were led home, their small faces sticky from a combination of hot dogs and cakes and their fancy dress wilting after all the hectic games. Some looked wistfully back as the teenagers moved in, relieved that they could now dance without the danger of stepping on tiny feet. Isabelle cleared up with the other women, glancing occasionally in Marcus' direction.

She was glad that he'd made friends and was enjoying himself. After a lot of dancing one of the older boys shouted for silence and out of the kitchen emerged Karen carrying the birthday cake.

Marcus looked at his mother across the room and mouthed "you horror" but his face was flushed with pleasure as he listened to the choruses of "Happy Birthday, Dear Marcus". Arthur and Lugh joined them at midnight, with all the other men who'd been working down the mine. Their deep male voices added a fresh burst to the energetic evening as they relaxed with cider or coffee whilst demolishing all the remaining food.

Lugh's main worry had been about the access to fresh water while the people stayed for any length of time in the mine. They had found the answer that night. A deep underground well. The relief that the men felt echoed noisily into the night.

She was glad that it was Karen's day for coming to Nodens. The previous night's celebrations had exhausted her. She watched Karen arriving through the gates and waddling up the drive. "Sam'll be up shortly," she puffed. "His tyre was that flat so he had to pump the old thing up again. Where's the boys? Still in bed are they?"

Isabelle nodded. "Sleeping like angels."

"Now I doubt if you'll find any Brussels sprouts finer than these," Sam said, leaning on his spade. "See that faint pink in 'em? Well, that's the bull's blood, they love it. Keeps them old pigeons away too." He rambled on as Isabelle dug up some parsnips for lunch. "You send Lugh or young Marcus after the hazelnuts, they're about ready now. Them old squirrels'll take the lot otherwise."

She felt a mixture of emotions about going to Bridget's place. Part of her wanted to stay with Marcus and watch the late film on television, part of her wanted to go immediately and start her preparations for the ceremony. Lugh watched her as she found one excuse after another to delay their departure.

"What's the matter, Isabelle?" he asked her as she found another thing in the kitchen that needed attending to. "Oh, Lugh, I don't know," she said, hiding her head inside his large jacket. "I think I'm afraid and I don't know why." He looked concerned.

"Is it because you're afraid of seeing the dead pass by?"

"I don't know, maybe."

There seemed to be a war going on inside her that she couldn't share with Lugh. He held her tightly, trying to break through this strange barrier that was keeping them apart, dividing their oneness. "Then you must stay here, if you're feeling like this."

"No." The voice was so strong. It shook Isabelle that she had made such a sound. "No," she said calmly, "we'll go, we have to."

They were already gathered together when she and Lugh arrived. The slippery tracks made walking precarious.

A fine rain sprinkled their faces as they struggled to the house. "Stop a minute, Lugh."

"What is it?" She looked at his face in the soft hazy light of the moon.

"I'll love you for all eternity," she said, reaching for his lips. They clung together, drowning in the torrent of overwhelming love.

The 'Brigit' was strong that night. Brigantia and Belisima sent every last ounce of energy towards Bridget as she led the ceremony. Healing spells were sent to those in need or in pain. Any obstacle in the way of the village's affairs was hexed. Prophecies flowed as the seeing eye revealed even greater visions. Then each one sat in the circle waiting for the departed souls to walk past so that they could wish them happiness on their journey.

She held Lugh's hand, her own fluttering like a small bird's as the first grey wisp took shape and walkened past them. The old lady walked slowly, her round face serene as she smiled at them, then continued on towards the waiting open door, leading out to the moors.

"That was Mrs. Bourama," Lugh whispered. "Her body housed the soul of Belisima." The next wisp was taking shape.

Isabelle suppressed her feelings of panic as she saw the growing outline of Chris. Her heart thudded as she watched him walk proudly past, not even acknowledging their presence.

Her head felt light and pains shot through her body as she watched him turn and wait for another wisp that was slowly forming. She felt the pressure of Lugh's arms around her as slowly the mist took shape.

She watched in fascination as her body's soul took the shape of Isabelle Carrington and walked quickly towards Chris. Behind her another shape formed quickly and followed in the shape of Marcus. The little family departed through the door, never glancing in their direction.

Another shape began to appear into a slim, beautiful young girl with long flowing blonde hair. Lugh moaned beside her as Erinna turned and looked in his direction before she drifted out through the waiting door.

MacOc greeted his returning older sister, Brigantia and his friend Lugh. They knew the time was coming closer and what their purpose was to be as the Celtic New Year began.

CHAPTER FIFTEEN

The wind pulled at her hair as she stood by the summer house and looked across the moors to the distant sea on the horizon. She breathed defiantly against the icy blasts, her nostrils flaring like a mare's as the shrieking draughts harassed her scarf and tried to pull it from her. She loved this weather, the force and aggression of its nature. She watched the trees bending and swaying, the dried twigs breaking away from the branches with the remorseless pressure from the elements.

The daring kestrel rode the currents of air, confident in his ability to play with the treacherous corridors of wind so long as in his heart he believed himself king of the skies. Brigantia felt an affinity with the kestrel as she watched him ride the heavens.

She knew that she, too, had many times over the centuries looked down upon people going about their daily lives and soared weightlessly as a spirit into the large ocean of the sky. Her strength had grown with each lifetime, with an evolving love that enabled her to embrace the world and every living thing.

She had shared that love with Isabelle Carrington. She had guided her through her environment with a stimulated memory, lit her path with intuition and warmed her mind to her soul. Isabelle would be reborn with purpose.

Love from Brigantia was not the false abstract love for humanity that successive power-crazed world leaders spoke about while hiding their personality defects from the people. Nor was it the hysterical euphoria preached to the people by religious zealots, sheltered from human contact by barriers of minion mystics. Her love was sharing human and spiritual strength with all living creatures. Allowing instinctive warmth and physical contact. Breathing into her soul the life soul of other people and giving them in return respect for their existence as humans of worth and dignity.

She wandered back to the house through the orchard, pausing to rest her cheek against an old apple tree. Valiantly, it tried to hold on to its remaining few leaves against the buffeting of the wind, its nude vulnerable branches reaching starkly upwards like placental roots to the womb-like sky. Which lifetime had it been, when a tree had so inspired her to start the long quest for truth? She touched the old bark, flaking around the aged trunk, and gently whispered her respect for its age and steadfastness. Young saplings were pretty and graceful but the old trees held the ground, giving shelter and fruit. The earth's very existence needed their experience of life and wisdom . . . as human society had once thought, before the insane cult of youth worship.

The pigs scampered through the fallen leaves that scurried like dried rustling crabs to form themselves into soft banks where small creatures could hide from the cold wind. Brigantia watched them with amusement as they rooted around for the stray fallen fruit.

Old Sam worked in haste to protect his vegetable garden, trussing, staking, and preparing his precious territory against pinching winter. The chickens shrieked with fright as the wind blew their feathers, forcing their plumage to resemble pitiful feather dusters.

She returned to the warmth of the kitchen and began the preparations for the Christmas pudding. The most important ingredient was love. This she added to all her Christmas preparations. Her wish, as she stirred, was for harmony in the home.

The others joined her in the traditional stirring of the pudding. Karen, Sam, and Lugh, each in turn, echoed their hopes for the community as they turned the rich mixture and wished.

Rosy-cheeked women bustled through the village. Spicy smells permeated the air as one family after another saw to the endless preparations for family reunions and joyful feasting.

MacOc returned to the fold, gratefully embracing the warmth and sanctity of the home and the familair friendship of his own people, the villagers of Athairton. The fir tree blazed with the light of the shimmering candles. Flushed, small faces stared in wonder as they danced around it to the accompaniment of the older Athairtons singing and clapping hands.

The old village hall's beams dripped with streamers and paper chains, glued together by small fingers in the village school. Games were played. The shouts of glee came from the young and old, whether passing an orange neck to neck or scrambling for the last seat in musical chairs.

After all the food had been eaten, leaving smears of melted jelly on plates, they all sat down to watch the children's play, joining in with hisses and cheers, as good challenged evil.

Brigantia sat with Bridget. The two of them content to be part of the relaxed, uninhibited family of Athairtonians who were exuberantly enjoying the annual production of St George the dragon. She looked around the innocent faces showing their enjoyment and smiled, remembering the stilted pre-Christmas parties that she had been forced to attend as Isabelle Carrington. There, people had hovered, ever watchful of the other arriving guests, the women's only passport to acceptability being carefully chosen words and the latest shade of lipstick. They had stood with heads erect like attentive chickens and scratched with lacquered nails thin fashionable cheese wafers.

She breathed in the warm smell of perspiration from Arthur's large frame, sitting beside her.

How different it was from the nauseating odours of wine mixed with mouthwash and nervous stomachs that had overwhelmed her at those horrendous occasions. There, the men stood decked in trendy shirts with carefully combed fringes over receding hairlines, thinking of their impotence and the ever-increasing money value of their spiritually empty homes.

The dancing was hectic. The tiny tots hung on to their fathers' necks, enjoying the steady rhythm through the security of the older stronger bodies. Singing and recitations wound up the evening, the last vibrations of gusty living sending them into the cold night air with the feeling of strength in unity with Dagda.

They came together, the family. The essential atom to the wholeness of society. Dagda enveloped the village in a blanket of fog which increased the feeling of being protected individual units.

What is a family? Brigantia watched the gifts being unwrapped. This family was united by a stronger tie than blood. It was linked together by soul. It was the unspoken understanding between strangers.

She looked across the flickering light from the hearth towards Bridget and smiled. The first quickening from Belisima fluttered insistently in her womb. And was this not the greatest gift of all, the gift of life.

The two women rested their heads against cushions and listened to the murmurings of family. Their two minds rested while their souls absorbed the sacred rays of the season, giving them strength and purpose. Their seeing eye surveyed the enigma of deceitful leaders debasing the symbols of their national flags. They watched the small communities of the world, striving to find their Athairton. People had yet to learn how to live in harmony with each other. And the prophets of that philosophy had always been ignored or persecuted.

Their souls felt their despair. They too, had tried violence in previous lives. How many times had they died fighting the Saxons, the Romans and other tribes. Each time they had returned to learn the lesson that sages had always propounded. The only way to true harmony was through self-knowledge and an awareness of the higher consciousness. Systems and dogma prevent the mind from reaching this consciousness and instead create ignorance, prejudice and fear.

Belisima whispered into their thoughts. "There will always be life. Life is the blood of the universe."

"Apple tree, apple tree, we wassail thee." The Athairtonians sang joyfully around the apple trees, remembering the magic of Twelfth Night or old Christmas Eve. The halo from the moon rippled across the sky like a disturbance in an inky blue pond from a bright pebble. Brigantia stood with Bridget drawing energy from the winter moon and sending their love towards Dagda.

EPILOGUE

She crept through the cow parsley on her hands and knees, her alert young eyes looking for the hiding grasshopper or a sudden spider. Smells of fresh grass and the soft warmth of the earth pleasured her senses. The sun beating down on her back heated the straps of her sunsuit as she explored the mysteries of the undergrowth.

She could see Daddy Lugh and her brother MacOc loading another truckful of things to take to the mine. Old Sam had taken pots of trees that she'd helped him to plant down there earlier that morning. Soon they would all go down, like they did every week, so that they could practise sitting in the dark waiting for the candle to be lit.

A bumblebee drifted past her and hovered over the clover. Chuckling with happiness she reached up with her small hands as he passed and tried to brush his softness.

She loved to watch them flying in and out of their funny wooden houses, stopping on the wooden shelf to play with their thin little arms before joining the other bees inside. Of course she knew all about bees inside her head, where she knew about all other things, but she couldn't say them yet because she'd only just turned four and she hadn't learnt how to say all the big words that could explain her understanding.

Mummy Brigantia knew though and Auntie Bridget, because they looked at her and she didn't need those words anymore. All she had to do was to think her understanding and they would reply with their thoughts.

She had told them yesterday that the truth of the world was beautiful and that reality was magic and of course they knew that too.

The speckled shape moved past the cow parsley and bellowed.

With tinkling bell, it lumbered towards Lugh and MacOc and the waiting truck. From inside came the sounds of the squealing pigs which made her laugh.

She loved the cow. She squirted old Mac dog with the soft warm milk that came out of the hanging things.

Daddy was calling her, "Come on Belle."

MacOc came across the field to pick her up and carry her. His beard tickled as he lifted her and placed her on his shoulders. She knew that today was the day they had always talked about. The day when they would have to leave, but she'd forgotten while playing with the grasshoppers. She could see her friends from the village, all heading towards the mine.

All the houses had boards over the windows like her house.

Watching the animals go into the mine reminded her of the Noah's ark that Daddy Lugh had made for her. Some of the grownups were crying which made some of her friends start crying with them.

She took a last look at the fields and the sun in the sky before she followed Daddy and Mummy into the mine.

She wasn't sad like the others.

She knew there would be a time of darkness but she was used to waiting in the darkness for the light.

Always she had to come through the darkness of the tunnel to find light and life.

ENDS

Before the Rain

*It is the 1960s, the days of
sex, drugs, rock and roll,
love and peace.*

*Four young women, Emmeline, Daisy, Sojo and
Marsha, travel from New York to England -
a voyage that alters all their lives irrevocably.*

*Thirty years on, Emmeline returns to stay with
Daisy - where it is with Daisy's children and their
'alternative' lifestyle that she feels most at home. Now
she must find a way to confront and purge the past, and the memories
which still haunt her of those first heady, blissful days in England.*

*A powerful, topical novel contrasting the teenagers of the 90s
with their parents, the original 'flower people' of the 60s.*

PUBLISHES 5th JUNE

Hardback 0 671 71868 1   £15.99

The Seventh Sunrise

The New Novel by

JUDY CORNWELL

Daisy in the BBC TV hit series
Keeping Up Appearances

Letting Go

*The secret is about letting go.
About knowing when you can no
longer hold on to something you
love dearly. About how you must
let go when it is time...*

*Anna, widowed, young and still hurting, has
become obsessed with her sick daughter, Sophie,
fending off everyone else and facing the strain alone.*

*When she meets Steve, a guitar maker, he quickly
becomes very attached to them. But before Anna can let
him into her life, she needs to let go of the past and its insiduous
influence on herself and those around her.*

*An enchanting mix of secrets, humour
and the complexities of family life*

PUBLISHES 5th JUNE

Paperback   0 671 85210 8   £5.99   'B' Format

This book(s) is available from your book shop, or can be ordered direct from the publisher. Just fill in the form below.

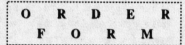

O R D E R

F O R M

Please send me...

TITLE

ISBN No.

SIMON & SCHUSTER CASH SALES
PO Box 11, Falmouth, Cornwall TR10 9EN

Please send cheque or postal order for the value of the book, and add the following for postage and packing:

UK including BFPO - £1.00 for one book, plus 50p for the second book, and 30p for each additional book ordered up to a £3.00 minimum.

OVERSEAS INCLUDING EIRE - £2.00 for the first book, plus £1.00 for the second book, and 50p for each additional book ordered. OR Please debit this amount for my VISA/ACCESS/MASTERCARD.

CARD NUMBER

AMOUNT £

EXPIRY DATE

SIGNED

NAME

ADDRESS